BLAAD

"a breath-taking adventure of a vampire who seeks his love"

A novel by Burak Cinar

ISBN: 978-137-08412-9-5

ABOUT THE AUTHOR

Burak Cinar was born in some year, in somewhere.

After completing his school life, he studied statistics, which was the department that he never wanted.

He continued his career in finance by having a master's degree in business administration.

He had a son whom he loved the most.

He now lives in Reading, and he loves there too...

(To contact with the author: burak81h@yahoo.com)

For my friends...

To let them learn the truth...

THE FIRST WORD

In fact, I was not going to write what had happened and I was going to keep them all as a secret…

I made a promise to myself...

But a few days ago, my other body, which was a vampire from a different universe, visited me and reminded me of many things I had forgotten.

I sat down that night with him and wrote this book as much as I could. I did not know what I was doing; the vampire himself could not make any sense, and rightly asked me why I waited for 11 years.

I could not answer, and I was not sure...

I just wanted someone to remember...

All of a sudden, I just wanted them to know the truth and remember their erased memories...

THE VERY BEGINNING

My House

The year 2005, the university was about to come to an end, and everybody, instead of planning a summer vacation, had started asking me the same question: "When will you do your house party?" That's because everybody who stayed at their homes through the years threw a small party, but it had not always been possible to come to my house because my house had never been vacant, and I was not living alone at my house at all! And perhaps because my parents were aware of the situation, they did not want to leave the house for me too!

But one day the big opportunity had come, and my father said to me: "My son, I have to go for a business trip for a couple of days, and your mother needs to come too, our home will be entrusted to you, do not call your friends in, stay quiet and let's find the house like we left it, meet with your friends outside of the house if you really want to, please..."

And just after my father had stepped out of my room, I took my phone with haste and I wrote this exact message to Monem: "May 17th, 2005, Tuesday night, my house, call everybody!"

The House Party

Shortly after my message was gone, the responses started to shed and the first message came from U: "Oh yes, of course yes!" And the second reply from Dhammal: "I am coming, my man!" Then the third reply from Behim: "Ooo Brother!"

That night passed quickly, and I was awakened early in the morning by a very energetic power that's been flowing in my veins… I waved my goodbyes to my father and my mother in the most prestigious and most comfortable manner, then I immediately ran to my green car to keep the school going. My purpose was not to catch up with the class, but to make announcements about my upcoming house party to my classroom and to my whole school.

I did not expect more people to come because the party was on a weekday, but I was very pleased to get answers to my question like "Yes!" and "We won't miss it!" and "Why not?"

I had invited my old friend and my classmate Aypher to take the course out of the classroom, and we got together to set up the environment. As my cousins Zjan and Kechuga were already at my home, there was not much work left for us, everything was almost perfectly complete. I was about to send a message to Monem that the preparations were near to completion: "The house is ready for party!" But then I realized that the house door was knocked, and the message was never needed.

The first ones to come home were my childhood friend Zegan and his brother Ouzan. The excitement was seen in the glowing eyes of the siblings entering the saloon with crisps and drinks on their hands.

When Zegan set the music to be played in the house, the door was knocked again and this time new lovers Hasun and Aijan came. Immediately behind them came the couple Boura and Guen, and both of the couples sat next to each other in the hall seats and had a good time with each other, drinking their beers and cheering happily.

The door was knocked one more time and a very loud and crowded group came in: Aridem, Airhan, Zumit, Zsami, Ahmun, Dijem, Sinuan, Zyleni, Hopuk, Sermut and Siertac... 11 guys, drinks in their hands, mostly beer bottles, and popcorns, cigarettes, crisps... Probably a mass massacre to the house would have had in no time!

Sermut, who dropped his crisps to the saloon carpet, when I lifted my single eyebrow, said: "We are gonna clean them, don't worry my dude!" He touched his oily hand on his head to have a scratch and this caused us to laugh all together. I said: "Have you all agreed and have you all decided to come at the same time?" The question was more echoed inside than a burst of laughter.

Everyone was welcomed, and while I was answering my phone calls and looking for Haipa, the skidding sounds from outside made me realize that Dhammal was coming. When I looked down from the window, I saw Dhammal, U, Behim and Monem descend from a single car, but Dhammal was going crazy, he was drifting his new car around the car park, oh dear, the real trouble was coming, but then thankfully he stopped and joined others, and when they saw me, all four suddenly started to climb up to the entrance of the house with a race.

As I opened the door and waited for my friends, I had my phone rung and I saw my soul mate was calling. My phone showed: ".Honey." and when I turned on my phone, Haipe said: "We're almost there my love. Hanpede, Jisemin, Soulqam and Ezma are coming with me too..." When I heard what she said, I was pleased with the reply: "Yes, of course they can come!"

When I turned off the phone, my friends and I were invited to the saloon, and they were inviting all of them to come in too. U said: "Kandaz lost the way, they were coming with Doan, they might be a little late than expected." Oh dear Kandaz, that's what I had thought, why is it always you when there is something fun and dumb?

Having invited all my friends to say, "Yes, and after Haipe comes, we will be all right." Then I have had a final look and made a quick calculation: "We'll be 32! Could the house be able to keep up with so many people?" 32 people! I was gonna get into real trouble, wasn't I?

The restraint of the door kept me from thinking about it and Haipe and our other friends had gone in and removed all the unnecessary disturbances in my mind...

The Party Starts

There was no need to declare that the party had begun; because everyone was hanging out, chatting, drinking, smoking, eating chips, laughing and most importantly having fun. I was glad only beer was the drink that was being drunk as I couldn't handle bunch of drunks if they were drinking real liqueur. Beer was enough!

Everyone was very happy, and it made me more than happy as well. I was the happiest to see my cousins and my friends were enjoying.

Everyone was in the house hall, and after a few hours of this, everyone got up and started to look at me with curiosity when I stood up with a great silence in the middle of the room.

- "Yes, friends, you know, there's a reason why we're meeting here tonight." I was standing there for a moment and I looked at everyone's eyes and made sure they were listening. They started to look at me one by one, eyes were getting ready for some excitement.

- "Because, the house is empty, buddy!" Sermut replied immediately with cheer.

Another answer, "That's right, buddy!" Was from Siertac sitting next to him.

- "Yes, the house is empty, but it may be full too!" The joke I made, created another big laughter again. The reference was coming to an old and very funny movie.

- "Anyway! I have one more good reason! A real one!" I spoke.

- "Again, Blaad?" Monem said, but everybody gave an empty look at him, but he did not mind.

- "Yes, again, what happens if we try it? Do we have anything to lose?" I asked the question to Monem.

- "What's the matter, my friends?" Ezma asked, looking for answers from Monem's eyes, and then she looked at me.

- "It is nothing but an empty legend!" U pointed out the one argument who supported Monem out with his hand.

- "U, today is May 17th and you know it happens in every thousand years! And it coincides with today!" My cousin Zjan tried to defend my thesis.

- "This is too cliché! Every thousand years, and coincidence coincided with that day." Guen said, gaining the appreciation of Boura in the eyes of many.

Haipe, who put the final word, "Will you tell us what is going on here now?" Cut the murmurs and made everyone look at me again.

I was about to start by saying, "All right, I'll give you all a quick summary. It is not something that occurs every thousand years, but still this is the day. Now let me explain." But Aypher and my cousins, except for the rest, had caused me to have a deep breath for a moment.

- "We're listening, Blaad! Come on, everybody, listen to him please! Nothing to lose, in fact, we can say, here comes nothing!" I got back together by the words from my encouraging cousin Kechuga, and I started to tell:

"My friends, you know that every planet, even every universe, or every plane or dimension, no matter how you say it, is said to have a parallel to every universe, and what would you do if I said it can be accessible from some areas in certain times? And that door or gate to a parallel universe will be open one day in which is today and that is gonna happen right now! Well, I mean, in a few hours! And where did I learn that from? This was just a theory we have learned from the conversation of two people, two shady figures would be a better definition, in the school, and one day we found evidence about it, a real fact, or could be a real fact, anyway, it is supposed to be happen just today and we are sure because of mine and Behim's calculation! The good news is that the gate, the actual gate, the antique fountain is very close to my house! This house! And, I say that at 12 o'clock noon, there will be a magnetic field next to the fountain, so let's try to get in if a gate to the possible parallel universe opens!"

Especially in this last culmination, it first caused a silence, then a big laugh.

- "Oh come on, leave it, is there an antique fountain really right down to your home, is it?" Asked U mockingly.

- "Okay, let's say these are real, what will happen if we pass through the gate?" Asked Zumit, again ensuring that all the heads turned to me.

- "How can I know? We haven't been able to test if before! How would we? But maybe today we can see it together? But according to what they say, you are replacing your equivalents that exist in the parallel world or dimension or maybe a possibility of your other existence... I mean, as an instance, in the parallel phase you are a policeman and when you pass the gate that police become you and your consciousness is now covering that character, or possessing it, and you are the person there." I tried to explain with my every possible knowledge.

- "Well, if they pass over here, while we are here too, are they becoming us? Or what will happen to us if they come here? I mean in terms of our existence. Will they become us?" Hopuk asked the question by lifting his eyebrows and added new values to the questions that could not be answered anymore.

- "I suppose it is so..." Said Zyleni, who thinks aloud, has already taken himself into the atmosphere of the event.

- "One more question, where did you hear it? What calculation, you mentioned about some shady characters?" Asked Haipe, to me and to Aypher.

- "You tell them Aypher." As I said, Aypher immediately coughed up his throat and hit his heavy foot to the floor as if he was getting ready for a fight.

- "You know we are a member of the Fantasy and Science Fiction Community at the school, and we have many books on this subject in our room. Anyway, one day when we were in the room with Blaad, we heard two people outside the room talking about parallel universes, and we listened to the door and heard what they were talking about... I think they knew everything and talked like they were sure and somehow; their voices were familiar; I mean we knew the voices... It was like me talking with Blaad..." Aypher paused for a moment and continued: "We listened to every word that were mentioned, and while we were about to open the door and look at them, they weren't there but we saw a book on the ground. We leaned over carefully and took the book, and while we were trying to find them and run after them, we realized that they were long gone."

- "What do you mean they were gone? Did you see anybody at all?" Asked Soulqam.

- "No, we saw them for a moment and then they were lost, but they both seemed very familiar..." I spoke.

- "Probably some of your silly friends who are joking with you... And where is this book?" Asked Ezma, and Behim started talking by showing the book to her…

- "The book is here, I've read it, worked on it, and if my calculations are correct, you know I never make any mistakes, only a few hours left before the gate is opening." Answered Behim, showing the book to everybody out of the bag beside him.

The book was as old as it was ancient, and among the yellowing papers, Behim's notes were visible. Well, not notes, but scribbles. Siertac was the first one commenting about the book.

- "What kind of paper did they use?" Siertac touched the book, "For the first time in my life I see such a kind of paper." He continued to talk.

- "Most likely they used human skin!" Said Hasun while taking a big sip of his drink and began to laugh. "And blood as an ink!" Continued with cheer, referencing the trilogy of a horror movie.

The book passed to everyone in the hall and a spot from Haipe made Behim and me embarrassed: "How did you find the exact date, and why do you think it will be a thousand years?" And look, 2005, Antique Fountain, it looks like it is your handwriting Blaad! There is no calculation here!" showing the handwriting.

- "Do you not want to do a bit of dramatization?" Aypher leaned forward, causing Behim to calm down, but no one understood anything and the growing question marks in their heads became almost visible.

- "Are you mocking us? Or deceiving us? I thought we were gathered for a party! Are you trying to scare us or something?" Guen came to her nerves. She looked around nervously and got up and sat down next to Haipe and began to examine the book quickly by turning the pages.

- "Yes, the exact date and place has already been given here, someone is joking with you." Guen, who scolded the book, angrily: "I do not see anything like it happens every thousand years, you always make up stuff like that!"

After these conversations, Behim put himself to his seat and took his phone and started playing with his phone as though he had never been there. I went to Behim's side and said: "Don't worry, we have done our part, we played exactly as we wanted, watch them now, they will propose to go there... Just to make sure if there really is a fountain, they will want to see it, just hold on." I sat beside Behim, taking the book from Guen's hand.

After a short silence, I wanted to do the next action before the atmosphere was gone, and I walked to the middle of the hall again with the book in my hand and raised the book to the air like a doomsayer:

- "Well, what are we doing now?" I started to look into everyone's eyes hoping for an adventure.

The enthusiasm of Aypher, who jumped to the foot, saying, "I say we go!" was evident in his glittering eyes. Zyleni followed him: "Yes we can go, it looks like a good adventure." He walked up to the foot and walked to Aypher's side. My cousin Zjan came to my side and put his hand on my shoulder.

Again, after a short silence, I made a sensible sentence saying, "Believe me, the fountain is right here, not even five minutes walking distance, and yet here we are, come on, at least let's have some fresh air! Let me at least show you the fountain." And everyone has approved what I said and started to collect their bags, and some grabbed their drinks to go out.

We were about to go out, but Behim's phone rang, and he said: "Hey friends, wait downstairs, we are coming down." And then he turned to me and said: "Kandaz and Doan finally made it!"

"Come on, let's go! All together!" Dhammal shouted, causing everyone to accelerate their moves off the house.

We went down in a large group and walked to the fountain between Kandaz and Doan's astonished gaze. Behim went to their side to explain what was going on to his friends. They were already up for some adventure, and they didn't complain.

We were about to leave the car park, and a car that was heading towards us caught our attention. It took me a while to get the sense that it was Mourem's car that flashed its long headlights in the darkness of the night, but their surprise made me happy. Moreover, after they parked the car, Dayra's, Meirve's and Foanda's trolling through the car added a different joy to all of us.

When my friends, who I have not seen many for months, got off the car and came to my side, there was Mourem with his crazy attitude asking the question "Did you really think a party without us? We have been waiting and waiting for this house to be vacated for ages!"

After shuffling and hugging, I mumbled, "36 people, oh my, I'm gonna die…" And nobody was able to give a meaning when I looked suspiciously to my house.

Meirve's question, looking at the crowd around her, "Where are you all going, why are you all out here?" Caused me to become serious and immediately pointed to Behim.

With the clear answer that I gave her, "Behim will give you a summary, we have few minutes, come on, a quick adventure before you party." and I made sure that my new friends were more than curious.

Behim, who started to tell the whole story, glanced at me in an inverted glance, welcomed newcomers and reminded me of the situation that he could convince anybody.

And together we started walking towards the antique fountain...

The Antique Fountain

After a short walk, we had a total of 36 curious people by the antique fountain.

The water of the fountain flowed slowly as usual, and the flowing water was beginning to accumulate in the pool of the fountain. The overflowing waters flowed equally downward from each side of the pool around the waterfall, and the person looking at it seemed to see their own reflection at the same time as a mirror...

Behim was the first one to break the silence while looking at his wristwatch: "Okay everybody, we have a time of maybe less than five minutes, enter inside the magnetic field!" Has caused everyone to shudder and some people started saying "Magnetic field" in a funny way, losing their attention, having fun of his words… Then I spoke: "Please guys! Let's gather around and stand side by side by the fountain."

- "Here comes nothing!" Added my cousin Kechuga.

After a few moments, the watch on the arm of Dhammal, which disturbed the silence, had blipped at noon, alerting us that the time has come. Dhammal, who kept the watch with his other hand, was trying to say something, but U took the word from Dhammal's mouth.

- "Look, nothing happened. Behim, you have made the wrong calculations!" Laughing, mocking Behim to make fun of him and to make him angry, as for some reason it was always U or me who enjoyed making Behim frustrated in serious circumstances.

- "Oh brother, doesn't it write in the book? The exact date and location? And I did not make a mistake, I do not make any mistakes!", Behim opposed U's words, took it personal and seriously, and began to look at me.

- "Or maybe this is not the fountain, not the actual fountain?" Continued U, trying to make Behim more frustrated.

But then, not only Behim, but all eyes turned to me. I tried to swallow: "Let's wait a bit... The magnetic field... The fountain..." I stammered and stared at Haipe for support. As Haipe responded by lifting her eyebrows, I began to think to take a deep breath and say something sensible.

Voices like "Let's return!" and "Shall we wait more?" and "Oh come on..." came from the group; but Monem, who did not look at me but concentrated on the fountain, yelled: "Stop it! Look!" and it caused all eyes turn to the fountain again…

And silence...

A great deep silence...

THE VISIONS

The Passage

The water that flowed through the fountain stopped...

More precisely, the water was hanging in the air...

When everyone looked at the mirror-like water, they started to see their own images more clearly...

Those are the ones whom they see; but their attire, their posture, their gaze and even their age were very different than now! They all looked at their different visions on the water.

Monem looked at himself at once. He had a long sword in his hand and glittered when he lifted the sword to the sky. But there was sorrow and pain in his eyes. Monem, who is not accustomed to see himself like this, squeezed his fists.

Dhammal looked at himself at once. He never saw himself fighting before. He took a deep breath, wondering if the blood on his face and body belonged to him.

U looked at himself at once. He couldn't see himself clearly and it was hard to see his hoody and shadowy appearance in darkness.

Behim looked at himself at once. The skeletal angry red eyes of his face were staring at Behim and it said, "Do not approach! Do not come!" Behim strongly shut his eyes without thinking.

Kandaz looked at himself at once. He saw a ghost screaming in pain. He was floating in the air, moving from room to room and looking for a way out. He wanted to scream, but he couldn't.

Doan looked at himself at once. He saw himself fighting, battling, and killing. Wanted a support and placed his hand on to Zegan's shoulder, located next to him.

Zegan looked at himself at once. He saw himself fighting, wounding, and killing. He wanted to respond to the hand touching his shoulder and put his hand on Doan's hand.

Ouzan looked at himself at once. He saw himself lying alone in a dark place without any hope. He took his other hand in a reflex to his bracelet and began to tighten his wrist.

Hasun looked at himself at once. The image of him in a very miserable state moaned: "Kill me..." He moaned again... One of the knees of him started shaking badly and he held to Aijan for not to fall down.

Aijan looked at herself at once. She saw anger. The fact that nothing could be done caused her to have more anger attacks. At that moment, Hasun's burden was felt in her arms and she struggled to keep her strength.

Aridem looked at himself at once. He saw himself running. Aridem, aware of the anxiety over the panicked image as his running, made it difficult to breathe.

Airhan looked at himself at once. He saw his inanimate body lying in a dark place and felt flocky.

Ezma looked at herself at once. The first thing that hit her eyes was some transparent wings. She seemed to be excited for a moment, but when she realized she was crying, she took a small step backwards.

Zumit looked at himself at once. He was on a horse, about to enter a war he knew he could not win. In the face of despair reflected from his image, his head leaned downward and found Zsami stood beside him.

Zsami looked at himself at once. He was on a horse, in search of justice, but his statement did not say so. For a moment he realized Zumit was approaching him and realized that he had the same feelings as him, putting his hand on his friend's shoulder.

Ahmun looked at himself at once. He was on a horse, looking for his king, helpless, lost his hope. He looked around and looked at Dijem, but he was concentrated on his own image as he could not see his friend.

Dijem looked at himself at once. He was on a horse, looking for his queen, in the sadness of not being able to fulfil his promise. He held Sinuan's arm very tight, but Sinuan did not even notice it.

Sinuan looked at himself at once. He was on a horse and was looking for his friends that he had lost. Then he saw his own dead body in the glimpse of an eye. An unexpected expression came into Sinuan's face and a few drops of tears came out from his eyes.

Sermut looked at himself at once. His already weak body was even weaker and the pits beneath his eyes were empty. There was literally no blood in his body, and his body was pure pale. When he saw the scars on his neck, he felt like he was losing himself for a moment. He tried to say something, but he could not find a reasonable word.

Siertac looked at himself at once. The lying image was coughing and was puking blood. His hand inadvertently went to his mouth, but he continued to look at the image.

Meirve looked at herself at once. Her hungry and thirsty figure was lying on a floor, she took her hands to her cheek and wanted to close her eyes.

Dayra looked at herself at once. She wanted to turn her head when she saw the image of her escaping and panicking eyes flapping like a bird, but she couldn't.

Mourem looked at himself at once. He wanted to scream when he saw his body lifeless lying on the ground, but he could not even find the power to breathe.

Foanda looked at herself at once. She fainted where she realized that her neck was broken, and she was about to die.

Boura looked at himself at once. He saw a king, but he was not happy. He was convinced that the crown on his head had no meaning. He noticed Guen's hand was reaching to him, the fingers crossed the gap first, but then he relaxed for a moment as he felt the hand of his lover.

Guen looked at herself at once. She saw a queen, but she was not happy. She saw the chains attached to her hands and hid her hands behind her back. She then gave her hands to hold Boura's hand and responded to the gripping hands.

Zyleni looked at himself at once. He saw a giant wolf attacking him, and his hands held his face in silence. When he saw his eyes, he noticed that his throat was about to crush by the teeth and suddenly he shut his eyes.

Jisemin looked at herself at once. She saw herself crying in the dark and caught by a wolf like creature. She shrugged her face and shook her eyes, hugging Hopuk.

Hopuk looked at himself at once. He saw himself fighting with a wolf, and then he saw the same wolf dragging himself. He snuck into Jisemin, who had wrapped herself on him, and continued to watch his image with complex emotions.

Soulqam looked at herself at once. She saw the ridiculously ranch, covered in a refreshment and felt wind in her face. Soulqam's knees were titled, realizing that there is something in the image that does not work out when she looked around with fear and anxiety.

Hanpede looked at herself at once. She saw her fluttering body on a furry creature. Hanpede, whose face had been cut off from fear, could not even move a muscle.

Zjan looked at himself at once. He was in a library and he was turning pages of some magical books in front of him. He could not find what he was looking for, he was continuing to translate the pages in tears. When he noticed the aged face of his own and pointed ears in the image, his eyes leaped from its nests.

Kechuga looked at himself at once. He was in a library, and his candle lit the room. His face was covered in wrinkles with deep thoughts. The image stopped and he said "Black..." to himself. "White..." Kechuga responded with astonishment.

Aypher looked at himself at once. The image was as dark as he could see the blood in his mouth and on his face. He took his prey that he had caught. When he looked more carefully, he understood that he was a werewolf, and his thrilling eyes shone.

Haipe looked at herself at once. She was flying in the sky with her pink wings, but she was striking to invisible barriers, and while she was about to fall, she was recovering, helplessly flying into another direction. She wanted to go to Blaad's side and tried not to look at the image because of the sadness she was seeing. When she noticed that Blaad was about to touch the mirror, she could only reach out her hand forward.

"Nooooo!" Shouted and screamed Haipe with her most powerful voice with all of her might as she could gather, but she noticed Blaad who was approaching the mirror. The whole group yelled, "No!" and "Don't go!" and "Stop!" and "Blaad!" Their voices raised and everyone was thrown forward to stop Blaad.

Blaad looked at himself at once. He saw power. He saw strength. He saw energy. He saw magic... Unlike everyone else, his face was laughing. He saw that the image on the other side looked at him and realized that he was showing his hand, welcoming him. Blaad did not hesitate, approaching the fountain. The image of the opposite said, "Come to me..." and smiled and showed his vampire teeth. This was more than enough for Blaad. He leaned his hand toward the fountain and his fingertips have touched the water.

And the time stopped.

Nothing was heard.

Everywhere was black.

Suddenly, it was like a fog, everyone was inside and whatever was that made everyone disappeared...

THE OTHER SIDE

The First Pass

The only thing that lifted Blaad to his feet, who found himself on his knees with a strange dizziness, was just his hunger. A hunger that he had not experienced before. It was like, he would have done anything just to satisfy the hunger. His eyes did not see anything. He did not care where he was or who he was.

He saw a body lying on the ground and felt warm blood flowing through the veins. He jumped on to the body and opened his mouth and drank the blood by splitting the throat of the person lying on the floor with his razor-sharp teeth. It did not matter what or who it was.

Blaad, whose apparition had disappeared and slowly came to himself, realized that the body belonged to his friend Mourem, the bloodless body lying lifeless in front of him. Without knowing how to feel, Blaad stood up quickly, clearing his mouth with the back of his pale hand, noticing the voice of the whimper next to him, and he saw a big black-haired creature.

He did not hear the screams around him, but he just kept looking at the weird creature as he measured whether the creature was a threat or not.

The creature looked at Blaad as well with confusion, then stood on the foot with his body resembling a wolf and thrown itself out of the place where he stopped and attacked to the nearest person at the back of Blaad. Foanda's cry came to an end with the creature's prickly teeth entering her neck and it began to crackle while the claws were pulling Foanda's heart out.

Everyone was panicking and screaming, and chaos dominated, and everyone started running somewhere.

An incomprehensible word of magic was heard, and those who realized that Behim had opened a gate ran through the gate. Behim turned his back to send a fireball to the creature backwards before crossing the gate. The fireball exploded by illuminating the environment, allowing the creature to howl in pain.

Another word of magic was heard and a group around it vanished together with this power word.

Watching the escape of the crowd, Blaad felt a pain in his face and noticed that Monem had sent a beam of divine light towards him. The pain grew even further, and Blaad found himself running away in the form of a mist which he did it by an instinct.

Blaad hasted and freed himself from the attack that was casted on him and after a long time of running away, he felt himself safe and took the human form again. He felt the tremendous stalks on his face and proceeded to the hill with cautious steps…

His instincts sent him to a castle like ancient building and he started approaching the gate of the castle, and he saw that the werewolf was also approaching to him from his back.

The werewolf slowly moved closer to Blaad and took the human form with pain and piled itself on the ground for some time to recover...

Blaad understood that Aypher was the creature himself and gave his hand to Aypher for help and lifted him up to his feet by healing his light wounds with a spell. The burnt skin of his friend was recovered quickly and for a moment Blaad realised he was casting spells without any effort but kept this thought for later to think about.

- "What happened to us?" Asked the vampire lord Blaad, feeling ashamed.

- "It was all real..." replied the werewolf Aypher, gaining his strength.

- "Hunger... I could not hold myself." Blaad shyly looked at his hands and then touched his teeth with his tongue to feel his weird vampire teeth. Then started looking at his friend.

- "Me too... The hunger! I couldn't stop myself. But where are we?" Aypher asked.

- "I do not know, but we will find out." Blaad replied.

- "How did you do magic? How did they do magic? Where did they learn?" Asked Aypher, shook his head and sat on the ground again.

Blaad thought for a moment and sat next to Aypher and kept looking at his hands. He realized that his hands were whitened but strengthened.

- "How did you know that you could turn into human form? Or to turn into the werewolf form?" Blaad began to talk. "Well, you know how to do it, so they knew how to do it as well."

- "It makes sense..." Aypher said after a few seconds, and turned his face to Blaad: "Are you really a vampire now?"

- "Yes, I'm the one I see in my vision." Blaad replied, and continued with the question: "Tell me about yours, have you seen yourself that you were a werewolf in your vision?"

- "Exactly just the same..." Aypher began to examine his wounds healing and closing like they never existed. "Healing spells?" Murmured but did not get any response as it was not a common thing for vampires casting healing spells.

Seeing that it was difficult and weird to talk, Blaad concentrated on himself for a moment and realized that he was not breathing. He seemed to be surprised at first, but then he remembered. A vampire would not breathe because the vampires were undead creatures. In other words, his body was technically dead… Because of this he had to pull air into his lungs to make his lungs work in order to talk, which was making talking much difficult and weird...

A few moments later of realisation of his nature and of the unfortunate happenings, Blaad jumped to the foot, shouting "Haipe!" And looked away and turned to Aypher with his eyes wide open.

- "Did you see Haipe?" Asked Blaad.

- "No, I did not see her, in fact I don't remember seeing anyone, all was blurry, actually I could not remember anything, I lost myself like I said before." Aypher replied.

- "I do not remember at all, everything happened so fast." Blaad said, and his face turned to the sky.

He took a few steps toward the castle's main gate and spoke to Aypher: "Come on, we shall get in, or do you have any other ideas where to start from?" Aypher did not object and stood up.

Blaad and Aypher walked side by side and stepped in carefully. The castle was very quiet, but when they entered the main hall of the castle, the castle seemed to have come alive. The candles inside burned themselves up and the doors that were closed were opened slowly by themselves, welcoming its owner.

While Blaad was checking the environment with his sharpened eyes, Aypher smelled the air, tried to hear any noise, but neither of them sensed any life forms or any danger.

Standing in front of a red door, Blaad quickly investigated the markings or runes at the top of the door, then entered the room and saw a shiny red dagger on the table. When he picked the dagger up to his hand, the dagger became very familiar to him. Blaad saw the inscriptions on it "RedBlaad" but didn't have time to pay attention and he immediately hung the dagger in his belt to examine it later and left the book from his pocket on the table near him. He checked his ring and saw a giant frame hanging on the wall while he was about to leave. When he looked at the frame, he was surprised for a moment, noticing that the portrait was empty, pitch black, then he walked outside of the red door to the large saloon again. Just before he left the room, his hand unintentionally touched the dagger again and a glimpse of memory appeared in his mind, forging the dagger with by magic, "How come?" Blaad thought, "Red is my favourite colour, but why RedBlaad, what does it mean, hmm…" He murmured to himself and stepped out of the room by leaving these thoughts away.

When he came out of the room, he walked to Aypher and showed him the other rooms: "There are a lot of space to explore. Let's explore if you feel good. Then we will go out to look for Haipe and the others." Aypher nodded and shook his head as an acceptance...

The Gate

"Inside!" Behim shouted, "Inside, quickly!" he showed the magical gate that he had opened and threw a fireball to the furry creature behind him so that it would not follow them.

The first person to enter to the gate was U, followed by Dhammal and Doan. Then Zegan passed through the portal door.

"I'm about to close it!" yelled Behim to Monem, who heard him while sending a divine beam to Blaad, ran to the door, and finally Behim stepped in and moved inward. The gate was closing so that Kandaz had to put himself through the gate, but only half of his body could enter the gate.

And the gate was closed.

Behim, who stepped in, said: "Are we that all? Was I able to save enough?"

Everyone continued to look at each other with puzzled expressions while the half of Kandaz was groaning and lying on the ground with a lot of blood. Literally, half of the body of Kandaz.

Everyone's eyes turned to Kandaz and they saw that Kandaz was cut from half. Kandaz turned his head toward Behim and gave his life by screaming with the last breath in his lungs.

Behim shouted "No! My friend, no!" and sensed Kandaz's disintegrating spirit and pulled the soul together with his hands and reopened his hands and sent Kandaz to the air as a ghost. "Least I can do..." murmured Behim to his friend who just died.

Kandaz first blew up with a scream, then sifted around all of them and disappeared from the eye through the walls, trying to destroy himself.

- "Was it necessary?" Asked Monem and continued "And now he is suffering more, why couldn't you let him die peacefully?"

- "What? Who are you to judge me!" Hissed Behim angrily to his friend, "How can you know?" Behim's face was darkened with anger and hatred.

They began to look at each other without blinking for some time.

For a while, the confused group that looked at each other, it became Zegan whom the first to break the silence:

- "Did you see Ouzan? Where is my brother?" Zegan looked around, asked questions, turned to his friends, but did not receive the answer he expected.

Dhammal asked a new remarkable question, "Where are we?" And he looked at Behim.

- "We are in a place like a chateau, the gate brought us here." Behim replied, glaring at the mirror on the wall and looking at himself in the mirror. He narrowed his eyes, glowing red, then closed and, thinking for a moment, said: "I am a lich!"

- "A leech?" U asked. Nobody was able to understand if he was asking this serious or mocking again.

- "A lich, a monster that defeated death." Explained Monem.

- "And how do you know so much?" Asked U without hesitation.

- "I must protect my soul!" Said Behim, heading for the chest in the corner, standing in front of the chest and murmuring again.

- "Protect your soul? You just said you were dead, what soul?" Asked U, losing his patience, looked at Monem to get a reasonable answer. But Monem just shrugged.

- "You wouldn't understand!" Hissed Behim with hatred and tried to completely ignore the disturbances.

- "Oh, you wouldn't understand." U mimicked Behim's words in a funny way.

Dhammal gave an end to the weird conversation and spoke while looking around the place, "Well, what are we going to do now?" He opened the door of the big closet next to him and saw the dazzling weapons in the cupboard and yelled "Arms!"

The friends who have made their way towards the armoury have examined the weapons for a while and started to measure their balances by taking the weapons that are best suited to them.

Monem picked himself a long sword, U took a twin dagger, Zegan and Doan took the broad swords side by side. Finally, Dhammal came, and saw the heavy war hammer, the greatest weapon of its kind, leaned his hand towards it bravely and took it among his strong and powerful hands like handling a light knife.

While Monem was acting with his long sword, it felt like the sword was a limb of his body, he was surprised to notice that he had been using this sword for years. The others had their weapons in their hands, and they all knew how to fight already. It was like they had trainings with those weapons for years.

U guessed, "And could there be any armour in that closet?" He went to the other closet and found out that he was not wrong by opening the door of the closet.

Monem, Zegan, and Doan began to dress up by choosing armour and shields for themselves. But Dhammal and U refused to wear any armour. Instead, U took himself a dark cape with a hoodie that would make him disappear in shadows.

- "I still cannot believe; how can these be all real?" Asked Zegan, who continued by saying, "We thought you were joking with us." He put his sword on his belt and waited for a reasonable explanation.

- "Believe me, we did not know, our intention was just to scare you and have fun. I have played with you since the beginning, but how could we know that it would be true?" Replied Behim in a dark tone.

- "What are we going to do now?" Dhammal was furious and repeated the question.

- "We will go out; we will find our lost friends and we will bring them here." Monem answered resolutely, slapping his shield on his back and struck his armoured chest with his right fist.

The actions of Monem's attitude added a moment of joy to the atmosphere.

- "The ring must be destroyed!" Doan spoke suddenly and everyone turned around and looked at him.

- "You have my axe! Well, or my war hammer." Said Dhammal giggling, understanding the reference.

- "A red sun is coming up; blood was shed last night!" U continued, and everyone started to laugh.

- "A toe story!" Doan carried on with the sarcasm… "If you know it, you know it…"

Behim, who is about to explode by rage, shouted: "Stop this madness! Our friends are lost or maybe dead! Beyond that, there is the body of Kandaz, who just died! And you can still cheer and laugh!"

Behim walked away from them and spoke calmly, "Go now..." Behind his side, he turned to Monem and said quietly: "Also, your presence is disturbing..."

- "Yes, yours too." Said Monem and he wanted to make an explanation without breaking his friend's heart: "I am filled with divine powers, and you are the death itself. Even if we are in the same side together, it is contrary to the nature, contrary to the rules..."

- "What rules?" Asked U, raising his eyebrows, still wondering how these two knew too much.

"He is right." Behim pointed the door with his hand and ordered: "You all go now!" When he realized that his friends were still looking at him, he repeated: "You may go so that I can make a plan!"

"But go where?" Was a question from U, while others were nodding to approve, they all have the same question in their heads.

"Just outside? It must be better than here!" Spoke Dhammal restlessly.

Monem looked at his friends and turned toward the door: "Okay, so let's go out! To find our friends!" He shouted. He was confident of his friends, and when he thought about it, his morale rose higher.

All of them suddenly went out of the chateau under the leadership of Monem and set out to search for their friends...

The Library

Zjan, who watched his cousin drinking the blood of a friend and did not want to get more out of this madness, saw the magical gate that was created by Behim next to him, but he concentrated on his own spell because he did not trust anyone else's magic.

His mind thought of his home but then the home became a library in his mind and began to cast words of magic to send him there. At the final words, he thought of the surroundings and changed some words to cover an area and closed his eyes and opened his hands.

When Zjan felt safe, he opened his eyes and saw a half body -which was only two legs- that was lying on the ground next to him.

Zjan seemed to be fainting for a moment, but then he nodded and continued to look around.

On the other side he saw Kechuga lying on the floor and his heartbeat accelerated. When he saw his cousin was breathing, he felt relaxed, but when he went to his side, he could not make any sense of the wrinkles on Kechuga's face, holding his hands with Kechuga's shoulders and calling it "Cousin Kechuga! Wake up! Kechuga!"

Kechuga came to himself, but he did not recognize the old, pointed-eared figure standing in front of him. He kept looking into his eyes and weakly asked, "Zjan? Is this you?"

Zjan nodded without speaking and made sure that Kechuga was safe, stood up to examine his surroundings, and noticed some of his friends standing in a corner and watching them cautiously.

Zyleni, Hopuk, Jisemin, Soulqam and Hanpede were there, and the five looked at Zjan with some disturbed gaze. Zjan, who narrowed his eyes, understood that they were staring at his ears, not at the eyes of him, and immediately his hands went to his ears.

- "It is real! It was real!" Zjan exclaimed and understood that his friends did not recognize him: "It's me, am Zjan... It's me, Blaad's cousin!"

Zjan's word "Blaad" caused his friends to feel more shivering and they came closer to each other as they have all seen what Blaad has become just some minutes ago.

- "No, do not be afraid! I did not understand what happened, I just casted a magic to save ourselves, and then we came here, and we found ourselves here! I just tried to save us." Zjan walked slowly toward his friends.

- "It was all chaos… Where are we?" Jisemin asked the question with a crying voice, giving his hand to Hopuk and asked for some emotional support.

- "We are in a place like a library, my love." Replied Hopuk and kept looking at her face: "You are also talking in an unusual way, that's different..."

- "Do not worry, I think we're safe here." Said Zyleni, staring at the surroundings, walked toward Zjan and tried to touch Zjan's pointed ears.

- "Safe here? There is a dead half of a body lying over there and you are saying we are safe here?" Cried Soulqam.

- "I didn't do that!" Replied Zjan while trying to avoid the hands that were examining his pointy ears, then tried to come up with something that would make sense, "I only teleported what was around me to a safe place!"

- "And we were around him… Right place, wrong time, or maybe right time." Explained Zyleni.

- "But where is my sister? Have you seen my sister?" Hanpede's eyes helplessly searched for Haipe, but no one could be able to answer the question.

The only thing that stopped Soulqam from shouting "I'm going away from here!" Was Zjan's words:

- "There is no door here." Zjan said, taking Zyleni away from his ears with one hand, pointing out the structure of the large room with the other hand. A building that resembles a library without doors, could it be creepier?

Soulqam, who whispered, "How is it possible?" Made it harder for her to comprehend the situation that they are in...

Zjan waited them to digest these extraordinary facts and answered calmly: "One can enter or leave here with great magic…"

- "Wait, have you been here before? How can you know? Why don't you then do your magic and let us go out!" Soulqam raised her voice.

- "Okay, but let's calm down and decide what to do first. And no, I haven't been here before, but I can feel it okay? And you saw what has just happened outside, let's wait here a little bit. Let's have some rest first. We are safe here." Zjan's calm voice tone made Soulqam silent.

Everyone looked around for a while and looked at the dusty books on the shelves.

Zyleni, who asked the question "How can you do magic?", had no intention of leaving his eyes from Zjan's ears.

- "I do not know; I can just do it." Zjan answered with a bored tone.

Another question came from Jisemin, "Why cannot we do it? Why don't we have magic?"

- "How could I know?" Zjan's answer was almost exhausted.

- "If you can do magic, why don't you heal Kechuga?" Asked Soulqam.

Zjan, who forgot all about his cousin, suddenly shouted "Kechuga!" and ran to his cousin who was still lying on the ground with half consciously.

He prepared his hands to cast a spell, but for a moment he stopped and turned to his friends: "I can't do any healing spells. I think I don't know any…"

- "What can you do then? You teleported us here but now you say you cannot heal someone?" Asked Soulqam furiously.

- "I don't know! Let me think." Responded Zjan, while touching his ears unintentionally.

When Hopuk heard this, he walked toward Kechuga and slapped Kechuga slightly. Hopuk slapped him softly a few more times and made Kechuga woke up effortlessly.

- "What happened? Water, please some water..." Kechuga tried to get up but could not succeed.

- "I can summon water!" Zjan opened his hands and spoke of a quick spell. Zjan, whose hands were filled with clean fresh water, made his cousin drank it from his hands. After drinking and spilling some, Zjan said another word and the water from his hands were disappeared. All others watched this by getting excited.

Kechuga, who regained some consciousness, could not take his eyes off Zjan and quietly asked: "Zjan, is this really you?" Zjan just nodded and leaned Kechuga on the side of the wall to rest, and added, "Just rest cousin, you will be fine."

Zjan turned to his friends and cleaned his throat: "Now we will all rest, we will think of the next step, we will search the library for answers, and we will make a wise plan. We can all go out together, but later..." He said, and he gained a big trust to himself in the face of his friends' heads looking at him with acceptances and more importantly with approvals.

Then he took a random book from the bookshelf and started to examine... He was as shocked as others but tried to mask his feelings and tried to remain calm as he saw that he was the only one with power, and he felt responsible over them. He wasn't sure if he could protect them all again, but he wanted to delay the going out and exploring option as much as he can. Another thing in Zjan's mind was, he needed to figure out why he turned into an old elf and why his cousin was also old but in a human form. He tried to get some sense out of the situation but everything that happened recently was very overwhelming and he knew the library which he felt very connected to it has some answers that he could get.

The Forest and The Castle

Another group that was not lucky as others were totally dispersed in the great chaos. The magic, the gates, the creatures, the blood, and the dying friends were enough to let go of their minds as if they were nothing at all.

Some ran towards the woods; some ran to the castle that appears from a distance...

Those who ran towards the forest were completely lost, and when their strength was exhausted, they rested on their backs.

Those who ran towards the castle were unluckier; because they had no idea that they would remain captive for many years.

Sermut and Siertac were the first to reach the castle. First, they looked at each other, then sat back, giving their backs to rest.

Sermut heard a voice which he had never heard in his life before and lifted his head upwards. He saw that something flying was approaching to them, and he swiftly stood up with Siertac.

Sermut's heart, asking "What the devil?", could not hold any more excitement and stumbled down and hit his head hard.

- "Stop! Do not come any closer!" Siertac shouted while trying to protect himself and his friend.

- "My friends, it is me, Ezma, it's me!" Ezma shouted down, landed, and united her wings behind her back.

- "What happened to you?" Siertac asked, felt relieved a little.

- "I do not know either! I looked at the flowing water, and I saw myself like with wings, then I found myself in the same way that Blaad touched the water, and I started to run away after seeing the massacre!"

Siertac calmed down and left Sermut's head with his hands at once, leaving one stick at hand. "Sermut! Are you okay?" He asked, but as soon as he heard other voices approaching them, he immediately turned back, leaving Sermut.

He understood that his acquaintances were coming, and he kept waving to Sermut.

- "What happened? Are you okay?" Boura approached the trio, speaking while he was supporting Guen who was clutching with one hand, and he was taking power from a long staff with the other hand.

- "We are all right, what happened to you?" Siertac asked.

- "I guess I just wrangled my leg while running." Guen replied.

- "Have you seen what happened to Mourem and Foanda?" Asked Hasun, approaching.

- "It was not as believable..." Aijan supported.

- "There is something very wrong here." Added Airhan.

- "My brother, is he here with you?" Asked Ouzan.

- "I don't think so..." Boura replied.

- "May they have entered the castle?" Hoping Ouzan and then he took a few steps towards to it.

On this last word they all turned their faces to the castle and looked at each other to be able to decide to carry on or not...

- "I think they entered the castle." Ouzan making himself sure of that decision and he sped up his steps and began running toward the castle.

- "We must carry Sermut!" Said Siertac and called his friends for help.

- "I am coming!" Said Hasun, went to Siertac's side and put his lying friend on Siertac's back.

- "All right, we can go in now." Siertac said and began to walk in heavy steps toward the castle.

The group, who had no choice but to go into the castle, walked very slowly. In order not to draw attention to the group, Ezma stayed behind them and walked very quietly, hiding her wings behind.

Once they were about to reach the door of the castle, Sermut lifted his head and noticed that they are getting closer to the castle: "No, not to the castle!" He shouted.

But it was too late...

The gate of the castle opened, and they saw the two silhouettes coming from the darkness were approaching towards them...

The Messages

Behim stayed alone in the chateau, sat on his seat, and thought for a long time. Then he rose to his feet and walked toward the armoured cabin, taking the red robe inside from the cabinet and studying it. He touched his fingers on the embroidered runes on the arms of the robe and wore the robe and looked at himself in front of the mirror.

He turned back to his seat and sat down, taking his head between his hands, and concentrating on himself. He then thought of his friends and tried to send telepathic messages to them.

He sent a telepathic message to Monem confidently, but when he was sending the message, he realized it could not reach him. Because he could only send messages to those who possess magic power like himself. Monem had magical powers, but he was divine, so he could not communicate with him because their classes were different. "Who else, who else... I don't think there is another lich in this world... But wait, does it have to be another lich, hmm..." Talked to himself quietly.

Behim tried to remember the day they came here. When Behim opened the gate, a friend who was standing nearby casted a transfer or a teleportation spell. He remembered, it was Zjan, another magic user. Behim tried forcing his powers to communicate with Zjan.

He focused on his telepathic powers and asked "Zjan?" And waited a response.

At the same time, Zjan was examining the books in the library and was looking for a logical answer. Just as another book was going to finish, a familiar voice calling "Zjan" echoed in his head and suddenly he stopped and listened to the sound. Once again it called "Zjan!" And Zjan first talked with his own voice, "Umm, who is that?", Then concentrated on his brain and telepathically replied, "Yeah?"

- "Zjan? Where are you?" Asked Behim, relieving that his attempt to communicate was successful.

- "Behim? Is it you? Where are you? We are in the library, but we do not know exactly where we are." Zjan replied, leaning back against the wall of the library.

- "A library?" Asked Behim.

- "Yes, we came here to heal up. At least we are safe here." Zjan said.

- "How many of you are there?" Asked Behim.

- "With me, we are seven." Zjan answered.

- "And another seven from me." Said Behim.

- "What about the rest of them? Or are they murdered?" Asked Zjan with shock.

- "There have been deaths, but most of them have escaped into the forest." Answered Behim.

- "Because of your games!" Zjan shouted, losing control.

- "No!" Said Behim and continued: "We were just joking with you! It was all a joke. If there is a murderer, it is not me! Their heads are on your cousin, Blaad! He is the one to be blamed, not me! He knew it, he knew it was all real and that's what it always was!"

Zjan did not respond for a long time. After a while, Behim sent another telepathic message:

- "We should look for a way out together... Are you listening to me?" Asked Behim.

- "I'm listening..." Zjan spoke quietly.

- "Then listen very carefully, since if you are in a library, check out all of the books and find useful information. How can we return to our own world from here, how we can turn everything back into original? How can we... Fix things…" Behim said.

- "Okay... We will try... That's what we are trying to do here too…" Zjan said, approving.

- "And do not go out, stay there in safety, stay there! Wait for my instructions." Continued Behim and stopped sending any more messages.

The frustrated Behim, walked a few steps, straightening the arms of the robe and looking at himself at the same time. When he realized that his face had begun to rot, he looked at himself more closely and hissed, "Blaad..." in hatred.

He then calmed his mind and concentrated on sending a telepathic message to Blaad. He called "Blaad!" And then again "Blaad!" Behim, unable to get any response, sat down on the couch and continued to think.

To the Captivity

Blaad, unable to find any useful information, ran into the main hall of the castle and waited for Aypher to join him. He was eager to go outside, but for a moment he hesitated when he felt the sun rising. Was the sunlight really harmful? There was only one way to understand it and Blaad, now exhausted, shouted: "Aypher!" He yelled and walked toward the main door of the castle.

"I am here, sorry but I have found nothing useful in the castle, actually I could not find anything at all..." Said Aypher, who came running. Blaad also added, "Exactly, this castle is empty but rocks!" and continued to walk towards the exit. He was determined to go outside no matter what would happen to him. Sunlight wouldn't be an instant death, would it? Or how worse could it be?

The castle's door was about to open, but a "Blaad!" voice echoed through his head. Then another "Blaad!" Blaad understood that it was the voice of Behim, paused for a moment but then ignored about the incoming telepathic messages.

Touching the castle door, Blaad seemed to push the door first, but then pulled back his hands and decided to step back a few steps before opening the door because of the sunlight.

He spoke a spell to the door, and the door slowly began to open. The rays of the sun came in and Blaad carefully stretched out his hands to the sunlight. He felt a slight burning as he thought, but the pain was reasonable and manageable. That is to say, he realised that sun rays would not have any effect other than the disturbing burning sensation. Blaad accepted this, smiled, gained confidence, and invited his werewolf friend by nodding his head to Aypher to follow him.

Together they stepped out and at the same moment as they looked ahead, they noticed that some of their friends were running towards them, or towards the castle.

Blaad saw Aypher transforming into the form of a werewolf and jumping towards the nearest target Ouzan and rushed towards Aypher at its fastest speed and stopped Aypher at the last second.

He turned the face of Aypher to himself and gave him an order: "Run to the forest! Leave us."

Having released, Aypher jumped over Ouzan and ran through the cries of other friends to the forest.

After Aypher left, Blaad said: "Welcome, my friends, welcome..."

No one said anything.

"You can come in." Said Blaad, looked at his hands, narrowed his eyes and looked at his friends again; because the rays of the sun that hit the surface of his face and hands began to discomfort.

- "Is my brother here?" Ouzan asked, looking hopefully at Blaad, and started pulling his wristband around his arm.

Blaad gave a clear answer, "There is no one here, except me." caused Ouzan to squeeze his face like a bitter lemon.

- "You killed Mourem!" A roar came from Boura who was approaching Blaad slowly while his face was turning red with anger and excitement.

Blaad shrugged his shoulders, saying "It was not intentional..." and he opened his mouth, took some air into his lungs, the lungs that he didn't need to use, feeling the blood in Boura's veins and having the fresh scent of it. He then regained his control and spoke calmly, "Let's talk inside."

Siertac shouted "You are a vampire!", left his friend he was carrying on his back, pointing to Blaad and yelling "Vampire!" Once more.

- "Well done! Wow! You are a smart one, aren't you?" Blaad laughed and cunningly continued: "Friends, I will not hurt you, please do come in, don't forget the werewolf may come back at any time. And I may not be here to stop it."

- "What's happening to us? Vampires, werewolves, fairies?" Sermut asked for help and gave his hand to Siertac.

- "Fairies?" Asked Blaad and Sermut's face turned to Ezma.

- "I'm not a fairy!" Ezma shouted, moving backwards a few steps, speaking, "Or am I? I don't know!"

Everyone's gaze was now on Ezma and it was a matter of time for Ezma to run away. Or at least she thought about running away or flying away. Instead, she controlled herself, remained calm and showed the crushingly beautiful wings, turned around herself and made everyone breathless. The two were up, other two down, symmetrically, four transparent wings coming out of the centre of her waist, the sight was magnificent...

- "That's just awesome..." Said Aijan, allowing Ezma to calm down and Ezma slowly hid her wings behind her back again.

While the group did not know what to do and what to say, all the faces turned to Blaad, who whispered "Sprite..." In the looks of curious faces, he continued, "She is a sprite, well, it is a kind of a fairy, in a better way..." Explained Blaad and examined Ezma more carefully. Blaad felt the flowing magic from Ezma's veins and smirked sneakily.

- "Okay, I'm going inside, come in, the door will be open..." Blaad turned back and entered the castle. His exploration could wait until later, for now the sprite was more important, or at least the pure and wild magic in her.

Watching Blaad's entrance into the castle, the group that had no other choice entered one by one with a glance and Boura was the last one to enter...

The Werewolf

The only thing that allowed Aypher to slow down the smell of human flesh. He was running like a crazy without getting tired and enjoying the wind that was hitting his face due to his super speed. He hasn't felt like this much freedom before, and the power of his body, especially his legs were supporting it better. But the smell was something that he knew he couldn't ignore.

Aypher suddenly stopped his run and looked around for the source of the smell.

He saw Meirve and Dayra, helplessly standing side by side near a tree. Lost from the group, knowing nothing about what has been going on, no idea of what to do... Aypher didn't hesitate and approached them slowly from behind. For a moment he stopped and was about to get away but then he did not try to restrain his hunger and jumped on them.

Aypher understood that they were as hungry as he was, but he did not empathize and thought only of his own satisfaction.

The girls who were panicked by the looks of their eyes were slaughtered on the spot by the claws cutting their throats, without even making a scream.

Aypher, who suppressed his hunger, lied on his back, and looked at the sky for a while. "I am the predator, and there is nothing wrong with that!" He thought, then moved on again and continued his run in the forest...

The Horses

The warriors that came out of the chateau looked like a small army. The swords, the shields and the armour were pounding as they walked, and all of these voices were making them enjoy all. Well, at least to the ones that wearing those.

- "We must find a horse." Spoke Monem, lifting his hand and pointing the long way ahead.

- "Right now, really? A horse? Do you know how to ride a horse by the way?" Dhammal asked, laughing.

- "Do you not know?" Asked Monem, causing Dhammal to frown.

- "Yes, I think I know..." Dhammal thought, so if he knew how to use his weapon, he wasn't surprised that he knew to ride.

- "Okay, but where do we find a horse?" Asked U. "And do we need only one horse or horses for everyone?" Winked with a cheeky smile...

Zegan, who suggested, "Let's go to the forest then." pointed to the trees on the left.

- "Do you think we will find a horse in the woods? Or horses?" Doan asked.

- "Yeah, there must be lots of horses waiting for us in the forest! Even maybe if we are lucky, we can find some unicorns or some flying pegasus..." said U mockingly.

- "We will find horses later. I think we should find something to eat." Dhammal said.

- "Hungry already? We haven't even walked a mile!" Objected U.

- "Okay, we go to the forest..." said Monem, the last point in the argument, and he started walking towards the forest.

The group left the road in front of them and walked quietly to the forest and stopped in front of the first tree.

- "We are going into the woods, do we agree?" Asked Monem.

U replied with a tired and complaining tone: "What difference does it make? It has been only a moment since we got out of that place, and you guys have all become needy; asking for horses, food, water, what else, women?"

Dhammal laughing "Ha-ha! Why not? And do you think we won't find our way in the forest?" and trying to cheer the group but couldn't succeed.

- "We all have bad nerves, you are right, but we have to find our friends…" said Monem, reminding them about their responsibilities.

Zegan said, "That's right. Friends first, food later." and he touched the wristband in his arm, thinking about his brother, and entered the forest.

With the silence they walked for hours without getting too far away from each other...

The Bay

Without looking behind them, the trio stopped by the excitement of finding a settlement, and they threw themselves around the soft floor and rested for a few minutes without speaking.

- "For how many hours are we running?" Zumit asked Ahmun, who was lying next to him.

- "I do not know, my friend, look at the sky, it is almost the morning time." Ahmun leaned over and looked at Zsami, who was trying to smoke his cigarette beside him.

- "Oh yes..." Zsami smoked the cigarette and stood up to look at the settlement. He sighed once more and gave his breath, saying "Oh yes..." again.

- "This man is smoking even here! Oh, come on!" Ahmun coughed by trying to stop the smoke with his hand.

- "What's wrong with that?" Replied Zsami by shrugging carelessly.

- "How come you brought that cigarette through the portal anyway" Asked Ahmun while squinting his eyes.

- "We are inseparable." Spoke Zsami again with his listlessly behaviour.

- "What are we going to do?" Zumit stood on the ground and started looking into the settlement.

- "I think we should try our luck with that small settlement ahead of us, maybe we can find an answer." Zsami replied.

All three quickly gathered up and started walking towards the settlement and leaned their heads above in front of the strange glances of the people. The settlement was tiny and reminiscent of a village. Even though it was early in the morning, maybe everyone was out and was working.

Ahmun shuddered for a moment, saying, "There is something wrong here."

"They're looking at our clothes or maybe your stupid face." Zsami giggled.

"Nothing funny about our clothes, but they do not even separate their eyes from us, literally." Zumit approved while trying to stay calm.

Zsami suggested, "Let's talk and ask where we are? Or maybe they know us already? Or maybe we are wanted?"

Zumit asked, "Will we speak in our own language?" He first laughed, then began to think seriously about what he said.

"Okay enough, stop talking!" Ahmun raised his voice, causing his friends almost jumping.

"What is it? Why are you shouting?" Asked Zsami with a loud voice.

"Friends!" Zumit shouted, "Do not shout!" He closed his mouth with his hand and wondered how they created a silly impression from the outside.

Ahmun asked, "Aren't they Boura and Guen?", and he pointed at the poster on the wall.

"Yes, they are... What does it say?" Zsami approached the post, reading the postcard: "Missing! Our King and Queen... " He said to Zumit and added," Look, it's written in our own language! I told you!" Later, he looked closely at the article but could not give any meaning to the characters he saw.

"The King? The Queen?" Ahmun approached the post board and examined the poster.

"What kind of game do you think we are in?" Zumit noticed the armed guards approaching towards them and laid his back against the wall saying "Friends... Look…".

The guards stopped in front of the trio and waited for a while, pulling their swords.

- "Who are you?" The first guard touched Zumit's neck with the tip of his spear.

- "We are Earthlings." Said Zsami, busting his chest and resting his hands on the waist.

- "You are what lings?" The guard looked at the trio with no sense at all.

- "The King and The Queen... They are our friends." Said Ahmun and the guards caused their grin.

Another guard said, "We understand, we will bring them in." He pulled the sword and pointed to the small building.

At the same time, the trio, saying "Why?", looked around with fear, but they could not find a solution other than to surrender, and they waited for the guards to lead them to the small building that resembles a hut.

The guards took the trio between them and took them to a pit-like building and closed the door behind them and imprisoned the trio there without making any explanation.

When the trio entered in the building, they saw another trio: Sinuan, Dijem and Aridem...

Now, the element of surprise was on the faces of the other three...

The Pink Wings

There was no concept of time and space. There was only nothingness.

Was she swimming or was she not aware of it? She could not understand if she was awake or not.

When an energy wave dragged her into an invisible barrier, she came to herself for a while and realized she was falling. She looked down with panic, but she saw that it was a non-typical, endless area.

As she continued to fall, she felt a surplus on her shoulders and noticed the new limbs she had never used. She knew that the feathered wings belonged to her and gave them a command with her brain, stretching her giant pink wings.

At that time, she came completely to herself because of the adrenaline and remembered her appearance in the vision. She waved her wings quickly, gathered her balance, and stood around for a while in the air.

With the excitement of using her wings, she flew to a direction in front of herself, but she was stunned again by an invisible barrier, making her start falling again.

She gathered her conscious quickly and started shouting "Blaad!" After shouting a few more times, she realized that her voice came too deeply, and understood it cannot be heard.

"What is happening? Where am I?" The voice of Haipe, who asked herself these questions, was hanging in the air as well as her body, in the nothingness...

The Dungeon

The group took strength from each other and walked into the main saloon, standing close, looking at the floor and the top which looked endless cautiously. The dull grey walls were very unnatural, and the aura of the castle not very welcoming, all was cold in it.

- "Has anyone seen Haipe? Or at least know anything about her?" Blaad's voice prompted everyone to shudder.

When no one ever answered, Blaad repeated the question and stood across from his friends.

The first person to say "No…" was Guen.

- "I did not see her either." Said Aijan and the whole group shook their head, confirming.

Boura shouted, "You owe us an explanation!", causing the group to become serious.

- "Do not worry, I'm just like you guys. I cannot believe it, too." Blaad shrugged his shoulders and continued: "But it's good, is it not?"

- "Is it really good? Our friends are dead, and others are missing! Haipe is missing! And you are saying this good?" Hasun shouted.

- "I know… But could you all stop shouting for a moment? When I say good, I mean it." Said Blaad, smiling with the vampire teeth. Then he lit a fire in his hands with magic, saying, "Yes, I mean it."

- "Send us back!" Said Sermut, walking forward.

- "Yeah! We want to go back!" Ezma supported.

- "You want to go back? Look what a beautiful fairy you are, what more would you ever want?" Blaad asked and added: "And I do not know how to get back to be honest. And, what made you think that I want to go back?"

- "No!" Yelled Boura, overflowing with patience, hissed, "If you don't bring us back, then I will make you bring us back!", he attacked Blaad and ran forward to try to hit Blaad with his staff.

- "Ha-ha! You will make me bring you back?" Mockingly replied Blaad and got himself ready to defend himself. It should be very easy to defend himself against unpowerful foes like that. Avoiding any miserable attacks like that were too easy for him and Blaad quickly stepped on his other side to dodge Boura.

Boura, bouncing back to a wall, fell on the floor, crawled on his back by trying to get up, and gave his breath and stopped for a second to recover himself by staying still for a few seconds. Boura's courageous attack which was not successful made the group took an organised position to attack Blaad, and this time it was Siertac who attacked Blaad.

Siertac took the long staff that Boura had dropped and turned it over his head and attacked Blaad, trying to hit him. Blaad did not spend any effort for dodging it but lifted his arm and the staff was easily broken on Blaad's arm. Siertac, who lost his balance, stumbled forward and Blaad, seeing the open-neck, could not stand it, grasped Siertac from his grotty position and pierced his teeth.

For Siertac whom he felt for a few seconds, as if it had been a lifetime, and that he had been drawn from the veins of blood. He wanted to get rid of it, but he was not able to find any power to struggle in himself, so he just let go.

- "No!" Shouted Sermut and jumped on Blaad's back and tried to pull Blaad's head with his hands to save Siertac.

Aijan, clutching the broken piece of the staff, quietly approached to Blaad and immersed the pointed end of the staff onto Blaad's arm with her very sneaky position.

Blaad surprised that the piece of wood hurts him, left Siertac and angrily turned to Aijan. His hand was going to slap her face, but he looked up at Hasun and he lowered the hand he had lifted and then spoke a quick spell and dazzled everyone's eyes.

Right after that, he thought of another magic to stop and keep his friends in line, and he scanned through his all the magic knowledge from his mind. The wisdom of a conjuring spell came to his mind and Blaad opened his hands to an empty space between them. The green lights flashing from his hands formed a light beam on the ground, and then two skeletons that formed and came out of the ground started looking at Blaad with empty eyes, waiting for orders.

Controlling the skeletons with his thoughts, Blaad directed them to the group that were still in unorganised motion and ordered them to arrest and neutralize his friends, without hurting them.

The skeletons looked straight at their targets with empty eyes and began to push them by just walking to them towards the dungeon.

Ezma turned around herself instinctively on the ground where she was standing on and spread dusts out of her wings over the skeletons. Her only intention was to defend herself and her friends and all she did was an instinct.

The skeletons were paralyzed for a moment with the influence of the magical dust on them, then they began to disperse and disappear.

"I do not know what I'm doing!" Cried Ezma, stood among the astonished gaze of her friends and started flying with her wings wide open. She only wanted to be free but couldn't see any opening so stayed in the air.

Blaad, who did not accept the defeat, thought more of a conjuring spell and casted it on to his friends in front of the line, this time a more complex spell of magic which took a few more seconds than the previous one. His hands started to glow in yellow while he spoke the magic words and his concentration was perfect while sensing his friend's movements.

A giant serpent started to take a form, coming through the yellow lights, and hissed and immediately attacked his friends.

Blaad's control on the giant serpent saved many of his friends' lives. At the last second, he commanded the serpent not to kill, but put them in a position to have control over them.

The control over the serpent worked as Blaad planned and wanted for. Blaad commanded the serpent only to make his friends retreat, pushing his friends back step by step towards the lower dungeon and closing them behind the bars as he wished, chained them to the wall with a telekinesis spell.

Blaad, who gave another command to the serpent, sent the serpent back to the main saloon and waited for the serpent to catch Ezma. The serpent crawled swiftly and looked around to find the last victim to be prisoned.

Having seen the giant unnatural serpent is coming for her, Ezma levitated herself higher and tried to spread her dust again from her wings. Ezma's dust did not harm the serpent much, but it burned the serpent's scaly skin. The creature was in pain which can be seen from its eyes and the only thing that prevented the serpent from killing Ezma was Blaad's exact orders.

When the serpent had enough of the dusts, it jumped up and got its victim and strangled her quickly, without doing any big damage. It fell back with Ezma and after a few seconds of struggle, the serpent started moving again and brought Ezma to the dungeon and dragged her towards the wall, leaving her to the empty cell.

Ezma regained conscious by having some deep breaths and started to look around while examining her body to find any damage but surprisingly she found herself unhurt. She saw Blaad is approaching him and tried to cover herself.

Blaad approached Ezma and chained her with a spell, glancing up at all of them, remembered Siertac was still upstairs, went back to the saloon quickly and found Siertac at the floor where he left him. Blaad stopped for a moment and examined if he killed him but saw that he was slowly and weakly breathing. He gently placed Siertac on his shoulder, then went down again. He left him in the cell with Sermut and turned to the serpent and thoughtfully spoke, "You may go now." and the serpent happily disappeared like resembling a fog.

Blaad shouted, "You did it wrong! You all did it wrong!" Blaad looked at each face one by one and said "I'm going to look for Haipe! You better get used to your new places!" He yelled.

The group that is left alone by the closing of the dungeon door desperately collapsed and looked at each other disappointed by their effortless failure without talking to each other...

The Orcs

- "What are these things?" Zegan asked, pointing to a humanoid creature they have been following.

- "How so? Do you really not know what we have been tracking?" Replied U.

- "Do you know?" Zegan surprised and looked at U.

- "Stop it! We need to follow it, just shush." Monem was serious.

- "And why are we following it? It looks like a scout, apparently going back to his camp!" Complained U while deflecting Zegan's questions.

- "Quiet!" Shushed Monem, lifting his hand. But Zegan was still not leaving U alone.

- "Okay Zegan, that's an orc, aren't you watching some movies at all?" U said and made Monem angry.

- "Are these orcs friendly?" Asked Zegan another question.

- "I did not see any good-hearted orc before." Replied Dhammal.

- "How many orcs have you ever seen Dhammal? And look, they also have food!" Said Doan and pointed to the bags of the orcs.

- "I'm attacking, then!" Said Dhammal and stepped forward with his war hammer.

- "Do not be silly, stop! They may be friendly too, we cannot know. But hey! Stop!" Monem blocked Dhammal and managed to stop him, but it was too late, the loud noises were enough to wake a dead up...

The Orcs heard the sound and they all started to search for the source of the voices, leaving their work or what they have been doing.

Because he did not want to fight for any reason, Monem stepped forward and crossed his hands across his chest, started speaking to the orcs: "We did not come for a fight. We come in peace. We're just looking for our friends."

Monem remembered from somewhere that holding his hands diagonally on his chest was a sign of peace, but it was not hard for him that the orcs to realize they were not familiar with this sign.

The orcs started screaming, gathering, grabbing their weapons, and started running directly to Monem.

The foremost orc noticed something like a flying hammer, but it was too late for him. The war hammer struck the orc's chest in such a way that the orc's feet were cut off the ground and the orc died before his body fell down.

U, who was already in a position of a double sneak attack, waited for the orcs to approach him and stabbed his twin daggers to the runner orcs into their throats without revealing himself. The orcs were suddenly destroyed before they saw what was attacking them.

Standing still in front of the runner orcs towards him, Monem lifted his shield towards the orc and stroked the orc with his sword, blocking its attack.

Zegan and Doan also rushed out of their places and attacked to the closest orcs. The duo, fighting in harmony with each other by giving the backside tactics, quickly killed three times more than the orcs themselves. They were fascinated by the technique that they have done.

Dhammal, who followed the last remaining orc who was trying to escape, held it with his bare hands and grabbed up by the head of the orc. He then lifted him up from his head and shrugged off the orc several times like crazy, then threw the lifeless body away with rage.

When the chaos ended, everyone looked around and they approached each other when they were sure that they had killed all of the orcs. Especially Monem's face was full of regret, and he was praying for forgiveness already. The adrenaline rush was over, but they were not sure if they did the right thing, apart from Dhammal who seemed to enjoy the bloodshed.

U, who asked, "Have you really killed all of them? Have you?" Caused Dhammal to laugh and to be proud.

- "Yes, they are all dead. We smashed them all! Oh yeah!" Dhammal proudly replied with a laugh, making U angrier.

- "Did you not think about leaving one alive?" U was very annoyed, and he kicked the lifeless body of an orc on the ground.

Dhammal's face was questioned, asking, "Isn't that what we were supposed to do?"

- "You have never watched a movie, you imbecile, you idiot! One should have been left alive and the questions are drawn! Do you ever know?" Yelled U with his most frustrating voice.

- "Then why did you kill those orcs?" Dhammal kicked another lifeless body of an orc that he had killed himself.

- "Okay friends, what's done is done, come on, let's check their bags, let's search for some goodies or some of their foods." Doan concluded the debate and began to walk toward the orcs' bags.

- "Good idea! At least some of us are talking sensible!" Dhammal said, taking his war hammer on the floor and following Doan.

After the first battle experience that they had gained, the tough group slowly threw out the lasting effects of the adrenaline that had spread to their bodies and began to examine the orcs' goods.

Monem said, "If you can find any maps, that will be much better…" and sat at the front of the camp where the orcs were found and set to watch their friends by deep thoughts… The funny image of Dhammal's tasting a possibly horrible beef jerky made him smile a bit.

The Non-Answers

Behim, following the ghost of Kandaz flying in the air with terrible screams above his head, stood out of his chair and began to concentrate and then sent telepathic messages to the library.

- "Did you find anything? Answer me!" The voice of Behim yelled at Zjan's brain.

- "Behim? Okay, it looks like there is not much to do here, nothing useful, but we couldn't even scan half of the library yet." Zjan replied.

- "It just doesn't make sense, why a library, why books, who wrote them and why? You have been there for some time, and you still haven't figured them out? And what do you mean there is nothing useful?" Behim's voice frustrated, freezing Zjan's blood.

"You must have also figured out the fact that I wrote these books, I mean my other self, as a librarian or as a historian, or as an archiver, or as a chronicler, or as a munimenter, or as a..." Zjan was also annoyed by the conversation and was hoping to end this.

"Enough!" Behim's extremely loud voice had a concussion effect on Zjan for a moment.

"What exactly are you after? What exactly do you want?" Asked Zjan, shaking his head.

"A way out of here! To return to the home, for instance!" Shouted Behim.

"We want that too!" Zjan said.

"And bring Kandaz back alive." Continued Behim while looking above his head, searching for his friend's ghost.

"Can we really do that?" Asked Zjan, hoping for something that would make sense.

"Yes! His ghost is with me. If I can get his full body, I think I might do something." Was Behim's reply which made Zjan worry.

"Please don't say you will animate him." Zjan was not sure how to convince him to let go.

"He was my friend! My friend! Not yours to decide! And Blaad will pay for it!" Behim was obsessed with revenge.

"It was not Blaad's fault that Kandaz lost his life..." Zjan's peaceful tone was too opposite to Behim's voice.

"If you oppose me, you will be the next!" Hissed Behim.

"I am only trying to help, and I will choose to be neutral as possible." Replied Zjan, making Behim calmer.

"I need my friend back, he is suffering." Behim spoke after a few moments of silence, making Zjan see that he is back to his senses.

"His other body is with me." Zjan said and continued before making Behim angry, "I haven't touched it but casted a spell that stops decaying on it, so yes, the other body part is here with me, in fact, I think I can teleport it to a location, or maybe to you..." The suggestion gave Behim a little hope.

"Fine, send it to me!" Ordered Behim.

"I will, but please be careful, think before you act, you wouldn't want to make things worse that is irreversible." Zjan was trying to convince Behim not to make thing worse as he knew it was Behim's soft spot when it was about Kandaz.

"I know what I am doing! Send it to me now! Behim was certain.

"Okay, hold on then, concentrate on the field that you want the body, and I will be able to do the transfer." Zjan was sure it can be done without any interruptions.

"Ready, do it." Behim concentrated on the empty floor that was right in front of him.

Zjan walked closer to the half dead body, took the image from Behim's mind, and concentrated on his spell while softly touching the body. The spell worked and the body disappeared like it had never been there before.

- "Did it work?" Asked Zjan but he already knew it worked, just making sure Behim was okay with that.

- "Yes, not leave it with me, go and find something useful!" Behim was done with this conversation and was too excited to work on Kandaz's body to regain his friend back to life.

- "I am trying, I told you, no useful stuff here like you asked." Zjan replied, hoping to get some understanding.

- "Then investigate further!" Said Behim, squeezing his fists.

- "Why are you not coming here?" Zjan asked, hoping for a negative answer in response to the question he just asked, regretting why he would offer something like that.

- "I cannot come! My soul is here!" Said Behim.

- "What soul?" Zjan asked but he already knew the answer.

Behim, saying "That's enough!", ended the conversation.

Behim, who was raged by the anger, threw a lightning bolt into the wall of the chateau, and tried to calm himself by listening to the crackling sounds coming out of the wall. He then looked at the lifeless body parts of his friend and started thinking about a solution. Kandaz and Behim were very close friends and seeing him like that was making Behim extremely sad. He had to find something to end his friend's torment.

A resurrection spell would have been the best if Behim had got some divine powers and for a moment thought about calling Monem back but then got rid of this thought as he was sure even Monem wouldn't have that much power. He needed a high priest for such a spell like that and there was not even one priest around as far as he knows.

Behim walked around the lifeless body of his friend by scanning his knowledge of magic in his mind however all he could have thought was reanimating a body as a zombie, or a skeleton, or a walking corpse. He had no knowledge of bringing back someone back from dead. What would have happened if he mummified the body and reanimate it as a mummy? The spells of necromancy would have worked but it wouldn't be his friend Kandaz who would have come back. The results would be more painful for both him and for his friend, so he decided to let him be as a ghost or a harmless banshee and carried the body parts next to the chest where his soul was secured. "The time will come my friend; I will fix this..." Promised Behim to his dead friend and walked slowly to his chair to think about a permanent solution.

The Freedom

Recognizing that his friends were bored and despaired, Zjan summoned another spur of sweets and offered it to his friends in front of him.

- "I do not want any more desserts! I just want to get out of this place! When will we go out?" Soulqam threw the book at her hand and tied the laces of her sports shoes which contrasted well with her clothes.

Hanpede whimpered, "We should go and look for my sister…" and gave a sad look at Zjan.

- "They are right, I think we should try to find our friends." Said Jisemin, backing Hanpede.

Zyleni and Hopuk also confirmed what was said and they all started looking at Zjan. The pressure on Zjan was heavier than before and he acknowledged the suggestions.

- "All right, all right." Zjan said, giving up and leaving the sweets on to the bookcase. "I'll send you out, but please be extra careful and take care of yourselves. Only walk around the library and do not separate and do not do anything funny." He spoke and continued with a little more thinking: "We do not know this world and we are not aware of the dangers of it. Be ready to face anything and if you see any of our friends, just take them with you and let them stay close to you. Tomorrow, I'll pick you up at this exact hour, too. I mean, I will teleport you back here. Understood?"

Everyone accepted this offer and gathered around Zjan.

- "How will you teleport us back?" Asked Zyleni before the teleportation spell ritual.

- "Don't worry, my spell will be staying on you, so it will be just a snap of a finger to bring you back." Zjan's tone made everybody relieved.

- "Let's do it then!" Soulqam was very excited.

- "Cousin Kechuga?" Zjan asked to his cousin who was sitting down in a close distance.

Kechuga coughed and slowly spoke, "I will not go, I cannot go…" He straightened his hair with his wrinkled hands and said, "I am not in a good shape anymore."

- "Okay, we will stay here, and we will continue to the investigation of the library... Let's see, take care of yourselves, and don't forget, tomorrow at the same time, you will feel a magical tingling feeling around you and know that it is me summoning you back here. Just don't go far, otherwise my spell might not work!" Zjan said, moving his hands and casting a spell and sending his friends out of the library.

- "Are you sure they will be fine, cousin?" Asked Kechuga just after their friends left the library.

- "They were so keen to go out, you saw it, I couldn't hold them anymore. And they are all adults so they should know better." Was Zjan's answer. "And now we can concentrate on you, on us, and find out the reason of why we are the only ones that are aged while others are in a very good shape!"

- "I know why cousin, it's the library itself, I can feel it." Spoke Kechuga softly.

- "But why? And why only us?" Zjan was not very happy about this fact which he was also suspecting.

- "It doesn't matter cousin, I am okay with that, just accept it and stay happy." Continued Kechuga.

- "I still need to find the reason cousin, maybe I can revert it, maybe I can…" Zjan stopped talking suddenly as he heard a weird noise that he hasn't heard before in the library, his sharpened ears were hearing almost every detail and this voice was very ominous. Was it from outside or inside or maybe in his mind? He was not certain but stayed alert by closing his eyes and only concentrating on his ears.

- "You felt it too? And you didn't feel where it is coming from, did you?" Kechuga was smiling to Zjan.

- "What is that cousin, what's going on?" Zjan was very anxious.

- "Touch the walls cousin, touch it, become one with the library, feel it." Said Kechuga while pointing around with his hand.

Zjan nodded and slowly walked to the nearest wall, touched it with the palm of his hands and closed his eyes. He felt like the library accepted his touch and was trying to communicate with him. Then he found out the source of the voice that he heard, he followed it with his mind and the image of a hidden room's door appeared in his mind. Zjan opened his eyes, he knew where he should go, there could have been answers, or at least something that he can lean on as it was calling for him… "You were right cousin, you were right." Said Zjan to his cousin, thanking him with his head, and quickly walked to the room that he saw.

The Barn

- "Welcome brothers, welcome, what a surprise!" Said Sinuan with a joy in his face and raised everyone's morale up.

- "Brother! What are you doing here?" Ahmun asked, as if he had not seen his friend for years, he ran towards him and hugged him strongly.

- "We didn't understand anything, once we stepped inside of the village, the guards captured us and locked us here!" Dijem replied.

- "For how long have you been here?" Zsami asked with a silly face.

- "We just came before you, are you joking or are you losing your mind?" Dijem replied with a half serious question.

- "Have you seen the poster of Boura and Guen out there? It said something about The King and The Queen." Ahmun asked.

- "We saw some paintings, but we could not read the details." Aridem said.

"Look at the horses!" Zumit said, showing the horses that were feeding and resting in the corner of the barn.

"There are six of them." Dijem said and continued, "The guards are really stupid, we can escape with the horses, can't they think of it?"

"How are we going to get out?" Zsami showed the door, pulled out another cigarette in his pocket, and lit it.

"What are you going to do when your cigarettes are finished?" Ahmun asked.

"We can find more... Can't we?" Zsami replied.

"Yeah, yeah you will find more, I am sure of it!" Said Ahmun, rolling his eyes.

Dijem wanted to add some joy to the atmosphere, saying: "It is forbidden to smoke in a closed area."

"Oh dear! Very funny! Very!" Was Ahmun's reply.

"Friends, how can you be so relaxed? Really, we are trapped, we don't know what is waiting for us and you are all joking, how?" Aridem asked and the seriousness of the group rose again.

"I think we can escape with the horses..." Zumit said, thinking up a plan and pointing to the door: "We can break it all together..."

Aridem, saying "Hmm, you reckon? Well, I guess it might work..." walked to the door and measured it with examining the door handles.

"Let's prepare the horses, get them ready." Ahmun offered, heading towards the horses, and one by one he began to untie them, while thinking loudly, "Why would they take us to the barn with horses, it doesn't make sense at all…"

"I don't care, okay, are we ready?" Dijem watched Zsami throwing his cigarette over the straws and raised his eyebrows.

"I want to make a flashy and unforgettable escape!" Zsami laughed and grinned and stood in front of the door.

Ahmun, who says, "If we cannot break the door, we will all get burn here!" Showed the straw that had already begun to flame.

"We will break the door my friends. We can do it!" Aridem encouraged his friends, saying: "Come on, we are kicking the door on three."

The funny group got tense and rushed to the door and jumped on it at the same time as Aridem's "Three!" and luckily the door got broken as expected and opened up by falling over.

Right after the heavy doors fall, they jumped on their horses that were waiting to be ready to run but restlessly because of the fire, and they all started to rush out of the barn which started to smell horrible smoke already and went full speed to the forest where they came from...

The Unknown

Soulqam began to run in the opposite direction of the library without looking back, feeling the freedom of the wind that hit her face. Her athletic body came to itself already and put on the brisk marathon with her untiring legs.

She just wanted to run without stopping. Freedom at its best. However, a large building, resembling a castle that seemed far away, caught her attention, she slowed down but continued her way, straight to the path of the castle, and ducked into the forest.

- "What are you doing? Stop! Stop!" Zyleni shouted several times and followed Soulqam for a while, but then got exhausted and gave up and said: "Well, I knew this... I knew she would run away!"

Jisemin, who saw Zyleni returning alone, was disappointed to see Zyleni's dull face and coming back empty handed.

- "Did she really leave us?" Jisemin asked and approached to Zyleni.
- "She left, of course, she was running so fast I could not reach!" Zyleni said.
- "Did she not know where she was going?" Asked Hanpede.
- "I do not think so, and how could she? She was just running away like crazy!" Zyleni replied.
- "That was not smart…" Shrugged Jisemin and accepted the fact that they lost her.

Hanpede, who murmured with tears, "My sister..." caused everyone to turn to her.

- "We'll find her, do not worry..." Jasmin consoled Hanpede's hands, comforting Hanpede.

When the group walked around outside of the library and found nothing useful, they sat on the ground together and began to think quietly...

Being a Vampire

Though the sun was right at the top, Blaad, running out of the castle, acted very swiftly and threw himself into the shadows of the forest.

He noticed a slight smoky smell coming from his hands which are exposed to the sun and from his face, but he did not care because he knew he could regenerate himself with a few drops of fresh blood, and he wanted to test his limits and see the consequences under sunlight.

He walked a little more, and suddenly stopped by noticing an appearance of a tiny, cute white rabbit in front of him. He kneeled and stared at the bunny, trying to be friends with it. Normally he was very good with the animals, but the rabbit began to escape without even looking behind it, sensing the pure evil. Blaad saddened for a moment in the face of this situation, accepting the rabbit's decision again and stood on foot.

He did not know what to do or where to go, but his priority was to find Haipe or at least a clue…

He thought he would turn into mist form and watch the environment from the top of the trees. But he remembered that his vision was limited when he was in the mist form and gave up on this decision.

He concentrated on himself to find out what other talents he had and realized he could levitate himself to the air. He opened his hands sideways and began to rise to the air, defeating his gravity. Uprising went up to the top of the trees, and when the rays of the sun struck his face, he closed his eyes and gave up on it as well and descended back to the ground.

He thought he could turn into a bat. It was like this in movies and in books that he read about. Some of the vampires that he read about could even turn themselves into a wolf or other creatures... He said, "Let's try the bat form first... Here goes nothing." and put himself in the form of mist again, and while he was going to be resurfaced, he managed to get himself into the bat form by thinking himself as a bat instead of as a human.

The bat, shaped in the air, fluttered before it fell, then headed to the top at a tremendous speed and flew over the trees and flew directly into the sky. He left himself unable to withstand the fluctuations of the rays of the sun for his whole body, and when he was about to fall again, he entered into the mist form again, he turned back to human form again, looking his back on and seeing the smoke spreading from his body, "That was too much exposure of sunray and now I really need blood if I need to carry on..." Blaad said to himself.

Blaad, convinced that he could not watch the environment without dark, went to look for hunting to heal his wounds. Could he have fed on an animal?

He pulled air from his nose and headed for the blood scent which he had smelled. A few minutes later he saw his devastated friends lying on the ground and whispered, "Aypher... What have you done; you monster!"

Looking at his friends' bodies for a few minutes, Blaad thought the dead blood could not be drunk, and gave up, not being entirely sure. Then it came to mind that he could reanimate them as zombies, but he could not find any purpose in that either.

Blaad, who was about to leave his friends saying "Dayra... Meirve... Forgive me...", became angry at himself for not thinking about it before when a crow was stood by the corpses.

Blaad casted a charm spell on the crow which was trying to eat some pieces from the corpses and called the crow to his side. Leaving the intestines pulled by the crow of the corpses, it flew and perched on the arm where Blaad raised. Blaad examined his charmed crow, then gave orders by his mind and sent it to the sky and began to watch the environment with the eyes of the crow.

He looked at south and saw his own big castle first. He then turned in the opposite direction and saw a chateau in the north. Turning to his right, he headed east and saw a circular structure which likened to a library. Finally, he looked west and saw small settlements like a village and released the crow by saying: "You may go now, you are free."

Leaving the charm on crow, it began to fly with high speed. Watching the crow, Blaad talked to himself again: "What kind of place are we in?"

"A castle, a chateau, a library, a village and a huge forest... It can't be everything, or is it? What a small world or a plane or whatever... But no Haipe…" He said to himself, and turned his direction to the west, and decided to follow the smoke coming from the village.

The Unlucky Six

The group's horses, along with the burning out of the ranch, were spectacular. It was quite easy to do the escape without needing to have complicated plans but just breaking the barn's door. They all rode their horses in a professional way that looked like a lightning coming out from the barn.

Some of the village guards went after them or some did try to put out the fire.

Aridem, who is at the head of the lead, shouted "To the forest!" and sprang the horse once more.

The long-running group slowed down while not being sure if any guards were behind them but took the risk and stopped to think about what to do or where to go next.

The first person to talk, "I say we look for Boura and Guen." was Ahmun while checking the way they just came, trying to see if they were followed.

- "I think if there is an answer, they have the answer as they are the answer." Zumit supported.

- "The king and the queen were on the writing, I did not understand anything, but it might make sense for us to find them..." Zsami, thinking aloud, put his hand into his pocket again and searched for another cigarette.

- "No, no more, enough cigarettes!" Ahmun said, approaching Zsami with his horse and hitting the cigarette packet and dropping the package down.

- "Stop, what are you doing?" Zsami was about to descend from his horse, because all the horses were scared at the same time, and he could hardly keep himself on the horse.

Dijem, screaming "Oh no!" lost his balance and started scrambling to the top of the scared horse.

Dijem, helplessly watching other horses started to run away, looked behind their friends, who began to disappear one by one, along with his own horse.

Three of the horses ran in one direction, one in a different direction and the other in a different direction, and they completely were out of Dijem's field of view.

Dijem noticed that his leg was broken due to the sudden falling over, trying to get up, but the pain on the left leg made him fell again with souring his face.

When he looked up and saw the familiar face, he understood what made the horses scared and turned them into crazy. The vampire, staring at the dripping blood on his leg, was approaching himself.

- "Just a few drops..." Blaad stood over Dijem's head and leaned over Dijem's neck.

What was the pain in the leg comparing this? Feeling the blood drawn from his neck, Dijem tried to push Blaad with his hands, but when he understood that he could never succeed, he surrendered and closed his eyes...

Blaad separated his mouth from Dijem's neck and pulled back his vampire teeth: "Sorry my friend, Dijem only a few drops of your blood... I had to…" But when he realized Dijem was already dead, he just cursed to his own will and got mad.

- "I must learn to control myself, I need discipline, an iron will!" Blaad continued to say this to himself dropping Dijem's body softly to the floor.

He looked at the ground and saw the pack of smashed cigarettes and drowned in his thoughts... They all were his friends, the friends that trusted him, and followed him. The pain was unbearable for a moment even though he didn't have a live heart that pounds, however his face was telling otherwise. Blaad was just standing like he was paralyzed and was thinking about what kind of a monster that he become…

Behind a distant tree, Soulqam, who could not believe what she saw and watched everything from the beginning to the end, seemed to puke first, but survival instincts got ahead and she recovered. She turned her sporty body backwards without making any sound and continued to run in the opposite direction...

The Magic Scroll

Zjan, who checked the time, went back to near of his cousin and asked if he needs anything. A shaking of the head from Kechuga stopped Zjan's enchantment spell.

Kechuga, saying, "I'm fine, do not worry about me. You may keep searching the room that you found." gave Zjan a relief and he stood firmly from where he sat and picked up another book from the library.

- "Here cousin Kechuga, another book for you then, and you know I'm always here for you." Said Zjan whose sharp eyes continued to scan the library.

- "Will you not take your friends in?" Kechuga asked.

Zjan, who said, "I am almost ready to take them in. Let's give them some more time, you know it hasn't been 24 hours in here yet…" excited to see them and hoped for good news.

Zjan, who took another dusty book with a white coat from the bookcase, saw a parchment in the space behind that book.

He immediately reached out and grabbed what was there and began to carefully examine the yellowed paper, which resembled papyrus, from behind the dusty books.

- "What did you find?" Kechuga looked at Zjan, trying to see the scroll.

- "Some kind of magic parchment... A scroll... It has my signature on it..." Zjan said, narrowing his eyes and continuing to examine the paper.

He studied, read, evaluated, translated, and took a deep breath to concentrate on messaging with Behim. Just before using his telepathic ability, he stopped and smiled to his cousin and said: "I am going to turn into a clairvoyant if I keep doing this." They both laughed to the joke which was maybe the first thing Kechuga ever laughed since they came to this place.

Zjan, who sent the first telepathic message, "I think I might have something to do with our goal..." started to wait for reply.

- "What did you find?" Behim's voice echoed in Zjan's brain.

- "A magic scroll..." Zjan said.

- "So?" Spoke Behim with patience.

Zjan continued explaining, "Plane changing, time bending, mind erasing... It's so complicated, there's a whole bit of everything..." paranoidly.

- "Hmm..." Behim started to think.

- "And I have my own signature on the parchment... And I believe this is the handwriting of mine. If it makes sense…" Zjan carried on.

- "Surely it does." Said Behim suddenly, "You were a mage here and you are now that mage! Focus on yourself, we need to find a way to make it work. We can fix everything with this scroll! And maybe we can even get back to our homes!" The excitement in Behim's voice gave hope to Zjan.

- "I'll work on it, give me some time... You know, these kinds of scrolls will destroy themselves after reading once. So, if you say that it can be done, we have only one chance." Zjan said.

- "I know!" Said Behim and continued: "That's why I will read that scroll myself after you study on it. You should send it to me after you're done! And not only that, maybe you should all come here too."

- "Okay, but as I said before, give us some time. Everything will be planned and will need to be on track. We cannot risk it…" Zjan replied, putting the scroll to his belt.

- "Be quick." Said Behim, terminating the messaging.

Zjan, remembering his friends waiting him outside and already late because of the scroll and his dialog with Behim, immediately casted a spell and sent himself out of the library.

He looked around... He couldn't see anybody...

The Outside

The group, whose nerves were already broken with the departure of Soulqam, could not find the courage to leave the environment of the library.

"This could be the Ravenloft World..." Zyleni looked back at the library and said, "No, no. I think we are in the Forgotten Realms... Could it be that famous library?" Then he examined the sky and said, "No, no, this must be Krynn! Look, there are moons, World of the Dragon Lance... Or is it not, hmm…" He spoke.

Zyleni was trying to figure out where they were together with the complexity of feeling, but he was not certain.

- "I think this place is a very unusual one... Extraordinary and different… It does not overlap with your ideas." Said Hopuk, who came near to Zyleni and put his hand on Zyleni's shoulder.

- "Oh, I do not know anymore..." Zyleni said uneasily.

A silly question of "Could we be in the world of Warcraft?" Came from Hanpede. Hanpede, who continued to say, "I played Warcraft in a lot of time...", looked at Zyleni with hope.

- "Yeah, and are we in a computer game? And does it really matter where we are?" Jisemin approached her friends and continued to look around with disgust.

- "Yes, it does matter! If we know where we are, we can behave accordingly and we can lead ourselves with caution! Not only that, I know about those worlds, well, more than you, more than all of you." Zyleni said.

- "Have you got magic? Or at least a skill that we have not seen?" Jisemin asked, putting her hands on her waist.

- "Friends, that's enough, it's a lot different than the places you know, and remember that all the worlds you see are fictional, so none of them are real! But if there is a truth, that's it!" Hopuk raised his voice for the first time in his life and ended the discussion with the logical statement he just made.

- "Maybe I do not have any magic ability, but I can craft a weapon!" Zyleni, spoke to himself, was a little farther from his friends and started to chisel a stick with a thick branch piece he found on the ground.

- "Good idea..." Said Hanpede, who found another stick and sat down beside Zyleni, followed by his movements, and started to chisel it.

Zyleni shook his head with the nerve of the situation and said, "We are not in a game, okay? And no, not like that!" He reached out with his hand to get the stick which Hanpede was carving, but Hanpede persisted not to give it and pulled it with her hands. Zyleni, who was standing still, hung out with all his strength and pulled the stick towards him. When Hanpede released the stick for a moment, the stick hit near the face of Zyleni, causing Zyleni to scream angrily and painfully.

Zyleni, trying to clean his blood with his hands, pushed his friends away who wanted to calm him down and yelled: "Leave me alone! Leave me alone!"

"I apologize, it was not intentional... So sorry about that!" Hanpede dared to approach Zyleni, but with Zyleni's repulsion she lost her balance and fell back on her back.

Jisemin, surprised by Hanpede's fall, shouted: "It is enough!" She screamed like a whistle and slapped Zyleni's face very hard.

Jisemin closed her eyes for a moment, waiting for Zyleni to be angry with her or with a slap, but when she could not get any response, her eyes slowly opened up and she saw Zyleni, standing in front of her, looking in shock. When Jisemin tried to understand what's happening, she noticed that Zyleni was not looking at her but her back.

Jisemin slowly turned her back, saying, "Something is behind me, is it now?" and saw the monstrous werewolf approaching them...

The werewolf was staring at the bloodshed over Zyleni's face and was taking the opportunity to attack.

The shouting voice of Jisemin, "Zyleni! Don't lose yourself!" Caused Zyleni to shake the horror off himself.

Jisemin, who stretched out on the chopped stick on the ground, took the stick into her hands with hope. But Zyleni came to himself and took the stick from Jisemin, pushing Jisemin up to the edge, trying to protect her. Zyleni: "Come on, Aypher, I know it is you!" Yelled and took a few steps forward, taunting the creature.

The werewolf did not need any taunting to attack. He had already taken the smell of the blood through the forest and ran straight to his victims.

Zyleni put his feet in a steep position in front of the creature to defend himself, but the werewolf has thrown itself onto Zyleni, breaking the stick by the pressure, and threw Zyleni over his back.

Although Zyleni managed to hold the werewolf's head with his hands, there was nothing he could do against the strong muscles.

Zyleni realised that his time has come as well, gave up and whispered: "Aypher... Please..." Causing the werewolf to stop for a moment, but the werewolf who had already lost himself with hunger, opened his mouth and attacked Zyleni's face and killed Zyleni on the spot.

With Hanpede's weak cry, the werewolf immediately stood up and turned back. He saw the group in chaos and decided to take them to an appropriate place to deal with them later.

The werewolf who put Zyleni's lifeless body on his shoulder, took Hanpede with a lap and held her on his waist and put the body on his other shoulder.

Jisemin and Hopuk, who were still in shock due to the death of their friends, were very easy targets for the creature as it grasped their necks without making any effort and began to walk towards the forest with his new victims...

A FEW YEARS LATER...

The Dust

Having completed his portrait with the finishing touches, Blaad turned his attention to the picture he had drawn and looked at the portrait for hours. Portrait had taken a full week from start to finish and he did not need to sleep or rest because he was a vampire, so he unceasingly finished his masterpiece, feeding on the prisoners he had placed in the dungeon and not stepping outside.

Blaad, leaving the dyes on the table, turned to the portrait, and asked: "Haipe... Where are you?" He casted an illustration spell to the portrait where Haipe's eyes were staring at him, and Haipe's eyes on the portrait smiled and blinked at Blaad. A sour smile came to Blaad's face, which gave him a fake joy in the illusion he made, but then his face suddenly hung up and he started looking at the book that was standing at the table next to Blaad.

He took the book, and when he looked at the pages, he realized that he had never studied the book carefully before. His eyes were overwhelmed to be able to examine the handwriting which was giving the coordinates of the location of the historical and antique fountain on the page of the book.

Recognizing the handwriting, Blaad shouted, "Aypher!" suddenly came out of the room with the book in his hand.

- "Aypher! Come quickly!" Blaad shouted again.

Aypher shouted back: "I am here... What happened?" Aypher came to the breathless Blaad's side and started looking at Blaad with eyes of asking questions.

- "Look at the book." Commanded Blaad and handed him the book.

- "The book?" Asked Aypher and took the book.

- "Look at the handwriting inside, that certain page with fountain. Does that sound familiar?" Blaad asked.

- "No..." Aypher said, curiously lifting his head, he continued to look at Blaad.

- "The writings in the book are my handwriting Aypher!" Blaad said with excitement and horror.

- "You wrote that." Aypher said, widening his eyes.

- "Yes! I am the author of this, and I gave the coordinates! But when could I have written it? And how has this book gone to our own world and how did it get to us... And why? More importantly by who?" Asked Blaad.

- "Those who left this book to us... They actually seemed so much to you and me..." Completed Blaad's unspoken words and there was no doubt in Aypher and Blaad anymore.

"I understand now. We were the ones who left this book in our world! But how? How can we go back and pass through our own world, and how can we do with these states? Or how did we know the date and the coordinates?" Blaad asked, but he did not ask it to Aypher and he knew he was thinking to himself.

"So, we found a way!" Aypher said and continued: "So we found a way to go back in time or pass our own world! Or sent our images, avatars maybe? But why... Why should we do something like that?"

"Some kind of a guarantee..." Said Blaad.

"A guarantee?" Aypher asked.

"Yes, that's what brought us here! And I have to learn that specific magic to do that!" Blaad raised his voice and headed towards the trinket.

"Well, will you send the book back? Again? Are we in a time loop? So many questions…" Aypher began to follow Blaad.

"Let's learn the proper magic first, then we'll think about what to do with the book. It is quite perplexing." Said Blaad and entered the dungeon.

The couple entering the dungeon passed in front of their friends' cells and stood in front of Ezma's cell door.

"Oh, is it my turn now?" Laughing Ezma reminded Blaad of his previous experiences and started looking at Blaad in a funny way. For Blaad, at one time, had tried the blood of Ezma and regretted as soon as the magical blood torching his lips and burning in his mouth and throat.

"No, I think I need your fairy dust this time." Blaad said, directly.

"Ha-ha! Why would I give it to you?" Said Ezma angrily.

"I knew you would say that! And I have no time to play!" Blaad said, lifting his hands and casting a spell of conjuration magic into the cell of Ezma.

In seconds, a skeleton formed within the cell that was standing on the foot and began to look around with empty eyes.

"Will you give me your dust?" Blaad asked.

"No!" Ezma yelled.

"Then strangle her!" Shouted Blaad to the skeleton.

The skeleton's dull eyes were shortened with the order, and it turned toward Ezma and began to walk on her. The skeleton, trying to hold Ezma with its hands, began to disappear when the wings of Ezma opened wide and spat some dust on it. At that moment, Blaad sent the skeleton in disarray and pulled the dust that was flying in the air with a spell and gathered them all in the bag that he was holding.

- "Thank you..." Blaad showed Ezma the bag and said, "You know I would never hurt you."

No sound came out of others... Two droplets of tears drooling through her eyes, Ezma sat at the corner of her cell and leaned her head forward.

Blaad walked to the exit of the dungeon saying, "I did not want it to be like this..." He wanted to say this to all of his friends, not just Ezma. And he had been saying the same thing to them every time he visited the dungeon. Blaad carried on walking to his werewolf friend with the bag of fairy dust.

The couple stood in the middle of the hall and started looking at each other.

- "What are you going to do with the dust? Are you mad?" Aypher asked, made Blaad's head confusing.

- "I'm not sure either, I just think it will strengthen my magic…" Blaad said, looking sceptically at the bag

- "If you say so! What are you waiting for then? Do your magic, look for Haipe and combine it with the fairy dust!" Suggested Aypher with enthusiasm and encouragement.

- "I think so too..." Blaad did not lose any time and began to cast a search spell for himself for Haipe When he was casting the spell, he opened the bag and sprinkled a pinch of dust in the air and began to watch the images that appeared in front of him...

The Nothingness

The oblivion that was there for Haipe had no bearing. She could not concentrate enough to calculate how many days or years passed. Maybe she was asleep or was she in a dream? She could not be sure.

She saw the spirits flying by, and she felt sorry for some, and smiled at others. She felt that she belonged where she lived. Maybe she was the oblivion herself.

The pink wings were never tired, if they leave themselves empty, they fall into eternity, even if they fly they cannot reach it once.

She knew she was in sort of a giant cylinder-shaped plane, but she had no idea what she was going to do or what her purpose was...

The Cousins

- "No, I cannot see anything. It's like a nothingness... Or... could she be dead? Aypher, do you see anything, or is it the same for you? Do you see anything?" Blaad asked, losing his patience.

- "No! Nothing!" Confirmed Aypher, but he had little hope of finding Haipe.

- "Do you remember the library?" Blaad suddenly asked.

- "Yes, which has no entry." said Aypher.

- "The place where you killed some of our friends." Corrected Blaad.

- "Yes... Sorry… I did…" Aypher stammered.

- "Anyway, you need strong magic to get in." Blaad smiled cautiously, pointing at his bag.

- "Could she be there?" Aypher asked.

- "She might be... And I'm sure I'll get some answers from there." Blaad replied and began to concentrate his transfer spell already.

When the magic was completed, Blaad, who sprinkled the dust on himself, hoping he would not share the same fate as the skeleton, but it was worth the risk.

The magic was completed smoothly and sent Blaad into the void and made him whole again inside of the library.

Blaad, shaped on the middle of the dining table, caused cousins to stumble on the foot and cough, causing their mouths to open wide.

- "Zjan! Kechuga!" Blaad shouted down to them and when he noticed that his cousins were trying to protect themselves, he hastily said: "I have not come to harm you! It's me!"

- "Cousin Blaad!" Zjan said, but his old face contrasted with this.

- "Oh cousin!" Kechuga ended the high tension of the environment.

- "What happened to you? It hasn't been that long, has it?" Blaad asked, looking at the old faces of his cousins.

- "We are fine, it is the library that is aging us, not the years…" Said Zjan, but Blaad continued to look at them with more questions but couldn't get any more explanations.

- "In here something strange happened for all of us... But you are fine, aren't you? So, you've been in the library from the beginning!" Blaad, in turn, embraced his cousins' hugs and began to smile.

- "Well, I saw what you could do, so I beamed some of us here." Zjan said, remembering what happened.

- "You can do magic!" Blaad exclaimed and asked, "Who else is with you?"

- "We were a total of seven... actually seven and a half... I mean there was a corpse that was broken up from the ground." Kechuga told.

- "Where are they? Is Haipe here?" Blaad asked, opening his eyes widely.

- "No, but Hanpede was here. Zyleni, Jisemin, Hopuk and Soulqam..." Said Zjan.

- "Then Zjan sent them out, and he couldn't find them again. They are all lost…" Kechuga continued.

- "What about the corpse? You mentioned about half of a body?" Asked Blaad, hoping the body belonged to somebody else.

- "It was Kandaz, not Haipe, don't worry." Replied Zjan, understanding his cousin's feelings.

- "So, you do not know anything about Haipe…" Said Blaad and lowered his shoulders with sorrow.

- "They went out to look for Haipe..." Kechuga said.

- "Except Soulqam, I know where they are…" Blaad talked quietly.

- "Where are they? Are they fine?" Zjan asked, feeling that his friends were crushed in the face of their responsibilities and hoping to get a good answer.

- "I do not know about Soulqam... But the werewolf killed the others." Blaad replied.

The silence that followed Blaad's words was probably the deepest silence that the library had ever seen.

- "I remember... The first day we came here. It was Aypher, the werewolf!" Kechuga spoke, in disgust.

Zjan, who says "Where is that evil creature now?", was burned inside to take revenge for his friends.

- "In my castle..." Said Blaad and Zjan's eyes leaped more and more from their nests.

- "How?" Asked Zjan without breathing.

- "At first, he had lost himself like me, but now he has discipline. He's actually helping me now. He is not going out of my word…" Continued Blaad.

- "I will kill him!" Zjan promised.

- "Yes, we will kill him!" Kechuga repeated, and nobody said anything for some time.

Blaad, thinking that it would be wise to take the subject to side to calm down his cousins, looked at the library and looked at Kechuga when he saw black-lined books and white-lined books in sequential order, said: "Black and white, cousin." and asked to his cousin: "You did that?" while looking at the books and Kechuga's "Yes, black and white, as always, has it been beautiful?" reply made them smile again.

"Fine, very beautiful... But have you had time to review these books?" Blaad asked.

"We literally looked at all of them." Zjan said and continued: "But most of these books tell the history of this place and the lives of people that we do not know. Each person who lived here has a book that talks about his life, and each place that has a history has also got a book that tells…"

"Okay, okay, is there any information we can find Haipe? Or do you have any kind of magic that you have developed so that we can find her?" Blaad stopped Zjan but asked with hope.

"No... I tried, but when I called Haipe, I saw only a void..." Zjan said, shrinking his lips.

"I cannot even see anything..." Blaad supported Zjan.

"But I found a magic parchment and I am working on it. When I'm done, I will send it to Behim." Zjan said.

"What? Behim? Do you see him?" Blaad's rising voice echoed in the library.

"Yes, I have communicated with him. I told him about the magic parchment and…" Zjan talked with a perfectly normal expression.

"Well, what does this magic parchment do, and why is Behim involved?" Blaad asked suspiciously.

"Cousin Blaad! With the magic that's written in this parchment, we will be able to return home. Besides, we will return to the day we arrived. And when we do, some of our friends will even be able to forget what happened! And if Behim is correct, they will come back to life!" Zjan said eagerly, but the suspicion surrounding Blaad's face began to grow.

"No..." Blaad said, "We will not return. We should not return…"

"Do you want to stay here?" Kechuga asked, entering the conversation.

"Do you want to return? You want to return that miserable life? We have what we want here!" Blaad said, exhausting.

"Cousin, look at me. We are in a library and there is no one else. We do not have any friends. If we go outside, I will not be allowed to walk. Maybe you have everything that you ever wanted but not me. I do not want to live like that." Kechuga proclaimed and he was very right about that.

"Well, to cast that scroll, what do you need to get it work?" Blaad asked.

"Behim wants some reagents and most importantly all our friends need to be gathered. When we finish working on the parchment, we will all meet in Behim's chateau." Zjan replied.

"Ha! Then there is no possibility. The magic will not work from the beginning." Blaad grinned.

"Why?" Zjan asked.

"How do we gather everyone? Some are missing, some are dead." Replied Blaad.

- "I do not know. Behim has the details, he is confident with it... And it should be enough if we have enough people." Zjan said.

- "Should be enough? Good luck to you then... There are things I have to do." Blaad relieved and leaned over the bag hanging from his belt.

- "Are you leaving us?" Kechuga asked sadly.

- "Do not worry, I will come again." Said Blaad and quickly disappeared by casting his spell...

Blaad, who was embodied in the castle, began to think about the conversations with his cousins while Aypher was staring at him with questioning eyes. Blaad then proceeded to his room without saying anything and began to think with the book in his hands and spoke to himself: "I see it now... I need to send this book back in time... I need to get this book to reach us... If the magic parchment works well as Zjan claimed, I have to guarantee that we can come here again..."

The Tasks

"And I officially declare you as the royal guards!" The headmaster shouted and continued: "From now on your first and only task is to find our long-lost king and queen!"

The applause from the crowd gathered in the square, and the cheerfulness of Zumit, Ahmun, Zsami and Sinuan, who were standing next to their horses, encouraged all the people.

When applause and whistling diminished, the headmaster turned to the other side and coughed and cleansed his throat: "And I officially declare you as the royal spies!" He continued: "Your task is to infiltrate into the castle and to kill the werewolf who is haunting us!"

There was a big applause again from the crowd. The faces of Aridem and Soulqam, who were not accustomed to such praise, were become red.

Years ago, the crazy group burned the barn of the village and escaped from there, but now they were leaving the same village with applause as royal heroes, and this time their friend Soulqam was with them who was found in the deep sides of the forest.

- "We were brigands but now we are in the state of heroes, my fine gentlemen... And Soulqam." Zsam said, looking at the village one last time.

- "Exactly! And I am lucky to have found you, too." Soulqam said and tightened the curb of her short sword on her belt.

- "We are both lucky." Said Aridem and gave Soulqam a pint of smile.

- "I wish Dijem was with us." Zumit said.

- "I wish that too..." Ahmun looked towards the road ahead.

- "So, now are we really heading to the castle? For our first official mission?" Asked Sinuan.

- "I think we should go immediately without losing any time. We have our weapons, armours and more importantly, our training…" Zumit said and touched his short, curved sword.

Ahmun shouted: "We will have Dijem's revenge!"

- "And then we can find Boura and Guen, our king and our queen." Zsami talked while packing his horse.

The crazy band that set out with great hopes, headed for the castle. They continued their way without knowing how much their courage and hopes will be useless against the inevitable...

The Components

Zjan, who sent a telepathic message "He came here! Blaad came here!" Slipped Behim out of his deep thoughts.

- "So finally, he could go out of his castle… So, tell me, what is going on?" Spoke Behim, with a mocking laugh.

- "He's looking for Haipe so badly, it's his only purpose." Zjan explained.

- "Hmm... And? Is that it?" Asked Behim.

- "He also saw the magic parchment." Zjan said, waiting for Behim to burst in anger, and thanked for the situation that he was not near him.

- "The parchment is still with you, is it not?" Asked Behim with his expected anger.

- "Yes, I do have it." Said Zjan and continued, without waiting a response: "I have the parchment, it is safe with me, but cousin Blaad did not think that it will work and also he does not want to return. In fact, he didn't seem he was interested in this scroll, but he seemed he was overconfident, nevertheless he could try to stop us..."

- "He cannot do anything... Did you study on the parchment completely?" Asked Behim trying to calm himself.

- "Little was left, but maybe, you need some magic components along with this scroll." Zjan said.

- "Maybe?" Asked Behim.

- "Actually yes, it would be better." Spoke Zjan, trying not to offend Behim.

- "What is it, what components? Just tell me!" Behim spoke again in anger.

- "Three components..." Said Zjan quickly and continued: "Tundra mushroom, blood algae and nox crystal."

- "Okay, leave it to me, I will gather the components. Go back to your work now." Ordered Behim and shut the conversation.

The Bundles

The guard duty was on U this time. While his friends were sleeping beautifully at the end of the camping fire which was almost extinguished, U ran around the camp and hovered around for any danger that might come to them.

"It must have been a mistake in order, I was keeping the watch the other day." U began to count the days with his fingers, but his blabbering increased as he calculated that he was unfair. "I need to rest, too!" He said to himself, and he shook his head and kept talking to himself: "And what could happen, for days, for weeks, we are wandering around without seeing anybody. And why did we leave the chateau again, there is nothing to be found, why are we outside again in the wild? I really need some rest!" He comforted himself a little more and laid his back on the back of a lawn.

He was about to close his eyes, just before he saw three objects approaching by flying in the air. These objects, resembling small bundles, were coming directly at them, and U jumped up off the ground and woke their friends up, shouting as if they had been swarmed by a giant dragon.

The shouting from U, "Beware, something is coming!", while pointing to the sky as if he was crazy with the situation, woke them all up.

Dhammal, who joked, "Is an object approaching? Could this be a fireball? Let's form the fifth element!" Laughed, but he narrowed his eyes and realized that three objects were actually approaching towards them when U pointed at them.

- "Stop it! Gather around me! What could these be?" Asked Monem, who immediately took his shield and formed a defensive position.

The group, trying to figure out what to infect them, the bundles approached into their fronts and fell down on their feet, before they even wore their armour.

- "What the devil? What trickery is this?" Asked Monem and looked at the bundles and casted himself a protective spell, taking the small bundle standing in front of him and opening it. A small note came out of the small bundle, and Monem began to read aloud:

Monem! Take your two friends with you and find a blood algae together! Put the component into this bundle that you found. This bundle will come back to me when the mouth of the bundle is knotted. A map is also here where you can find the blood algae! After that task, come back to the chateau! We will be able to return to our homes! Behim."

When Monem finished reading, he put the bundle and note into his pocket and started looking at U. "Okay, I will read it." Moaned U and opened another bundle that he had taken, and began to read:

"U! You need to find a nox crystal! Put the component into this bundle that you found. This bundle will come back to me when the mouth of the bundle is knotted. A map is also here where you can find the nox crystal! After that task, come back to the chateau! We will be able to return to our homes! Behim."

U looked at his friends not knowing what to say in response to the task, and finally Dhammal opened the bundle which had fallen to the bottom of his foot and began to read:

"Dhammal! You need to find a tundra mushroom! Put the component into this bundle that you found. This bundle will come back to me when the mouth of the bundle is knotted. A map is also here where you can find the tundra mushroom! After that task, come back to the chateau! We will be able to return to our homes! Behim."

Dhammal, who recovered the note and the bundle with his big hands, could not say anything, and added the note and the map between his stuff.

- "It says we can return to our homes..." Repeated Dhammal with a whisper.

- "We have to do these tasks as requested." Said Monem grieving and looking at the hanging faces of his friends.

- "Are we not going to do this in a group? Are we not?" Asked U.

- "No, we will do as told. This will be a short separation for us both, but we will meet again in the chateau as soon as we send the components back." Assured Monem.

- "It's not going to happen! After all this time, all together, I don't want to be separated!" Said U angrily.

- "Why did you say so? It will be fine!" Assured Monem.

- "We have no idea what to do or where to go. Find this, find that, put it in the bundle, so what? Will I go to the chateau and wait for you? Or will you wait for me? Maybe it will take me a year to find this stupid component, but as for you only a week? In the rest of the time, will you sit in the chateau and wait for me? This is absurd!"

Monem interrupted U's words by saying "Dude..." and put his hand on U's shoulder and said: "Do no worry, we will meet again..."

- "I think it's worth trying... He says we can go back." Said Doan.

- "Right..." Zegan silently supported.

The shouting "Well, if you want to leave the group so much, then good luck to you!" came from U the he quickly checked his daggers and disappeared into the shadows in seconds.

The group looked at each other desperately, but it happened. Everyone turned to Monem, and they waite for a word of encouragement from him. But, at any time and in all circumstances, overcoming courage Monem chose to remain silent this time.

- "The order came from a great place, guys! Let's crack it up, and there's a long way to go." Spok Dhammal's dull voice, and everyone started looking at Dhammal.

- "As you wish my friend." Said Doan and gave his hand for a handshake.

Dhammal said: "I'll be seeing you as soon as possible." And accepted the handshake.

- "I would say be careful, but should I say that to your enemies?" Zegan said, allowing the group to hav some laugh.

- "Have a nice trip. We will wait until the morning. Then we'll hit the road." Monem said and gave a ver strong hug to Dhammal.

- "On the fifth day of the dawn..." Dhammal started to humour but could not bring anymore laughter as i was the time for goodbyes.

- "I'll see you soon my friend." Smiled Monem, understanding the joke.

- "See you all soon..." Dhammal said and started to walk to the north…

The Guards

The guards who stood still before the castle stopped their horses with Zsami's crying, "Stop!" and they a descended from their horses.

Zumit, who said, "Tie the horses and do it very tightly!" recalling previous experiences.

- "I think we should tie the horses altogether too." Ahmun insisted.

- "Good idea, so none can escape." Said Sinuan.

The guards who gave their decision, tied their horses to the trees nearest to the castle, and began to walk towards the main gate of the castle.

- "So, are we going to knock the door?" Aridem asked showing the big door.

- "Yes, what else can we do?" Zsami said.

- "So, if the werewolf opens the door, do we say we are here to kill you?" Soulqam asked a sarcastic question.

- "No, okay, we did not have a proper plan, but as I said, we have training, the discipline, weapons, numbers, so, yes we can say we are here to kill you and we shall kill it." Said Zumit.

- "There are six of us, it has no chance." Sinuan encouraged his friends. They all were very overconfident.

Ahmun said: "We will kill whoever comes out of the door immediately! And avenge our friends…"

With Ahmun pulling his sword, the whole group pulled their swords and waited to reach the door first. With Aridem touching the door, the castle gate was opened to the rear and the group was shuddered by the cold, unnatural and chilling air flow from the inside.

A figure who walked slowly through them from the inside of the stall, stood right opposite the guards and started looking at them unresponsively, raising his face to daylight.

As expected, seeing a non-attacking person leaving the castle was a disappointment among the guards, but the suspicions about the identity of the person came to an end as the figurine breathed in a resemblance of a wolf.

Before turning to his werewolf form, Aypher spoke, "Welcome and now say hi to your deaths!" and within a few seconds he transformed into a werewolf.

Ahmun's reaction was in haste, and he tried to pierce the werewolf's stomach by making a quick stabbing attack with his sword. He used both of his hands and the power of the acceleration of his body, but he felt like he hit a rock. He realised he didn't deliver even a minor damage to his opponent and tried to defend himself instead of performing another attack.

The werewolf who laughed at him saying, "Only silver can harm me, you ignorant idiot!" struck Ahmun's face along with his throat with its left claw and threw Ahmun back in blood in a few seconds.

This important point that the werewolf said was made the whole group upset as no one had any silver weapons and because of that important fact the group could not find the courage to attack again.

The werewolf evaluated the distance from his enemies and jumped on the nearest one and shook Zumit from his shoulders. It was one of the creature's favourite attacks as it was bloodless yet effective.

Recognizing that a burning lighter came on him, the werewolf returned to Zsami and said: "I am not a troll you fool, and that little fire cannot hurt me!" He then pressed on Zumit's lifeless body and jumped on Zsami, biting Zsami's throat with its teeth, puncturing it and killing another guard.

The werewolf, who saw Sinuan trying to escape without looking after him, began to pursue Sinuan. But Sinuan was not fleeing, he was running to his bag on the horses and trying to get the silver blade out of his bag.

Sinuan finally reached his bag and managed to grab his silver blade and tried to aim the creatures head to make a hit with it, but he needed a bigger one to hurt the werewolf. Accepting the hit to his face as a crumple, Aypher howled with pain but drew Sinuan's knife-holding hand with its claw and pierced its teeth to Sinuan's throat with rage, cutting off Sinuan's head completely.

The werewolf, who sensed Soulqam, ran towards her with a big anger out of its eyes, suddenly thrown forward to her and he was ready to overthrow Soulqam and wanted to hit a claw to her. When the creature's talon was about to descend into Soulqam's face, a pale hand gripped the werewolf's arm and blocked him to do that.

With the voice of Blaad, saying, "Enough slaughter, that is enough..." the werewolf stopped its attack, and Soulqam, who knew the owner of that hand, thought that her life was saved, or she was heading towards a more delicate end.

Soulqam clutched her hand to Blaad's holding hand, started looking at Blaad without saying anything. Her death was perhaps in a moment, but she did not want to feel that she was afraid. If she meant to die, she would die in honour!

When the werewolf began to collect the corpses that he had killed and drag them towards the forest, the vampire and the new slave were left alone.

"Do you know where Haipe is?" Blaad asked first, but Soulqam just shook her head from side to side. Blaad, saying, "Come with me." grabbed Soulqam from her arm and started walking to the castle together...

When the gate of the castle was shut and the werewolf were far enough away, the horses in the forest calmed down and another horse started to run away from them in hurry. Aridem, who had watched everything, had a single thought: "He will gather all the guards he can find; he will arm them all with silver swords, and strike them directly to the castle and destroy everything!"

The Plans

Being sure that his friends had taken the bundle packs, Behim started to take his impatient steps in the chateau. Then he sat down on the couch and began to concentrate on sending messages to Zjan.

Behim's voice echoed in Zjan's brain, saying, "The magic components will be here soon!"

"Great! And when it's all set, we'll beam into the chateau with the parchment." Zjan said, squinting his face.

"Yes, as we agreed." Confirmed Behim.

"What about Blaad?" Zjan asked.

"He must be here with us, too." Said Behim.

"How will it be? What's your plan? Apparently, we cannot just invite him." Asked Zjan.

"Do not worry, I'll send him a message and tell him I have found what he wants the most." Said Behim, giggling.

"It will only make him more furious… But hold on, you said he was not getting your messages!" Zjan said with a rebellious tone.

"We'll see! Otherwise, I'll find another way to bring him here!" Assured Behim.

"But he will try to stop you for casting the magic!" Zjan objected.

"I planned it too. I will call a creature from the darkness and attack Blaad. While Blaad is dealing with it, we will have already casted our magic. If this does not work, I will ask for your help." Behim continued: "And I will change this magic a little bit... So be here as soon as I summon you, do not make any delays!"

"Okay, we'll be waiting for your call. But watch out, you can kill all of us by trying to change the magic even a little bit." Zjan said uneasily.

"That's why I have to study the parchment too! Be ready and come here when I call you!" Shouted Behim.

"Okay, will do..." Zjan said, ending the conversation.

After these conversations, Zjan thought whether he was on the right path or not and began to walk in the library with holding a candle. "I hope he's correct..." He said to himself and added: "We have to try it because we have to get back to home, we have to take this risk, we have no other choice..."

The Terms of Agreement

Blaad and Soulqam walked into the alley and walked to the main saloon. When they were in the middle of the hall, Blaad released Soulqam's arm gently, and Soulqam had to rub her arm with her other hand.

- "So, all my friends are teamed up and they all want to kill me." Blaad said.

- "No!" Shouted Soulqam and Blaad was surprised by this unexpected shout.

- "What do you mean by no? You were right here at the door! You've waited for this day for years! You did not even say hello!" Said Blaad, slightly lowering his voice.

- "No, listen, we actually came here to kill the werewolf, but the werewolf attacked us in the first place." Said Soulqam, trying to dominate her voice.

- "If you come down to the castle door armed, and attack, what else did you expect?" Blaad said.

- "We were blind, made mistakes... But my friends' main tasks were to find the lost king and queen." Soulqam tried to explain and thought of how foolishness, how her friends just died in a terrible manner and looked at Blaad's face with a small hope of understanding.

- "How did you survive?" Blaad wanted to change the subject.

- "Long time ago in the forest, in the library, then the village... Long story short we lived in the village..." Soulqam summarized.

Blaad, waiting for the continuation of the story, stayed still without saying anything. Soulqam was apparently thinking of her deceased friends with tears, and she noticed a cold change in the atmosphere.

- "They were my friends too..." Blaad said suddenly.

- "I'm sure it was!" Said Soulqam in disdain.

- "They would have been alive now if you had not come here. The werewolf only hunts if anyone comes near! He never attacked any village!" Said Blaad and the debate was over.

There was still a deep silence and the pressure continued to get higher.

- "Did you say something about a king and a queen?" Blaad asked, starting a new topic.

- "Yes, Boura and Guen." Soulqam said, ignoring.

- "Well look at that! You really mean it? Boura and Guen as in king and queen?" Blaad asked, struggling not to laugh.

- "Yes they are! Or they were! Why?" Soulqam asked, frowning.

- "Are they king and queen? Very good!" Blaad started laughing.

- "What's so funny?" Asked Soulqam, annoyed.

- "They're here..." Blaad pointed to the dungeon with his hand.

Soulqam's eyes grew big enough to come out of their nests, repeating: "Are they really here?"

- "Come, I'll show you, come on..." Blaad said, holding onto Soulqam's arm and pulling her toward the dungeon.

The couple entered the dungeon and stopped in front of Boura and Guen's cells. Soulqam saw two curls of sadness in front of the scenes she saw, and she checked the iron bars of the cells containing the people and tried to calm herself down.

- "What have you done, Blaad?" Soulqam whispered.

- "I did not do anything. They did that to themselves." Blaad approached the cell and began to look towards the king and the queen.

- "What is it? What do you want?" Boura shouted from where he sat while trying to remember who the new person was as she was the first new person that they were seeing after years.

- "My king..." Blaad laughed, then returned to Guen and added, "My queen..." and he laughed again.

- "That's right." Said Soulqam, responding to the insubstantial glances of her friends and continued: "You are the king and the queen of this realm... Everyone out there is looking for you."

- "What? We?" Guen asked unbelievably.

- "Well, apparently you don't know much but everyone has a role in this world... So, your task was to be the king and the queen, makes sense now." Blaad said, cutting off laughing.

- "Release them please." Soulqam said, "All of them, please..." And pointed her hands to the entire dungeon.

- "Not yet... But we can make a deal." Blaad said, holding Soulqam's arm again, and they sneaked out of the main saloon together.

The couple, silent for a few seconds in the middle of the hall, entered the red door with the guidance of Blaad. Blaad showed the portrait on the wall to Soulqam and explained the terms of the agreement: "You will be back to where you came from now, to your village or whatever it is that you are calling. Everyone in the neighbourhood will try to find Haipe. You will find her, and you will bring her to me, right here...

Neither I nor the werewolf will attack you, and after that we will never be exposed to each other. I will also release all our friends, including your king and queen, except Ezma. That's our deal."

Listening to the deal and recording all the details in her memory, Soulqam looked back at the portrait. It was uneasy as she bit her lips, and she had difficulty believing what she heard. She was sure to die a moment ago, but now her knees were shaking unintentionally by the excitement as she was going to be free again very soon.

- "Will they believe me?" Asked Soulqam, restraining her vibrating body.

- "If you want me to come with you." Blaad grinned.

- "No, no." Said Soulqam for a moment as she was still shaking and threw her hair back with her hands, making her neck unwittingly open.

- "I think you need proof for that!" Blaad said, quickly pulling Soulqam with his hands and putting his teeth around her neck.

Perhaps experiencing the recent events that had happened within a few hours that should have happened for a lifetime, Soulqam was able to resist the pain with the impact of the shocks she had embraced and succeeded in pushing Blaad with her bare hands.

- "You can resist... You are strong..." Blaad surprised and released Soulqam.

- "Why?" Soulqam asked with touching her wounded neck with her hands.

- "Here's your proof." Blaad talked clearly.

- "Am I going to be a vampire like you now?" Asked Soulqam quietly.

- "No, it needs a different ritual to become one. And you wouldn't want that, and also I wouldn't want that." Blaad smiled.

- "Okay..." Soulqam shook her head slightly while touching the spot on her neck.

- "Go now." Blaad said, pointing to the door and continued: "Go and tell them what we talked about, what we agreed on. If they find Haipe, then we will honour the agreement."

Soulqam asked, "What about the werewolf?", remembering the dangers outside.

- "Be sure that you will not get hurt, trust me. Just find Aridem and go with him." Assured Blaad, with the most confident tone of his voice.

- "Aridem! He is not dead, is he?" Exclaimed Soulqam.

- "No, I saw him with the horses, and made sure he wouldn't be hurt by the werewolf. Now go, trust me." Spoke Blaad.

- "Yes, all right, I'm going out now." Said Soulqam, turned back and started to walk slowly.

Soulqam, still unable to believe that she was alive, was in great perturbation with every step towards the door. As if an assault would come from behind any moment, her thighs stood up and her muscles were involuntarily shaked. When she approached the door, she turned back for a moment and looked back. When she saw Blaad standing still in the same place where she left and calmly watching her, her body felt a relief. She walked right to the door and accelerated her steps. Soulqam, who went to the sunshine from the open door, started running without looking back...

The Chains

- "I will break these chains!" Boura yelled, behind the leaving couple. Then he tightened his chains and pulled them. He tried to chisel by rubbing the floor and the wall. He was even angrier at the desperate gaze of his friends and began to hit his chains on the iron bars of the cell.

Hasun, who was in the near cell, called: "Do not tire yourself, king, we will never be free again."

- "We'll get out of here!" Answered Boura.

- "You're trying for nothing, my love..." Guen quietly said.

- "Do not lose your hope!" Boura shouted angrily and everyone stopped murmuring.

There was no hope that anyone would be able to escape.

And Ezma's "Hope is something to reject the truth…" words caused everyone to shudder...

The Community

Aridem, who stood for the last time on the war techniques of the guards, wanted to say a few encouraging words to them. He cleared his throat and went ahead of the guards. He was about to start talking, followed by the sound "Aridem! Aridem!" running towards them, he noticed that Soulqam was approaching, and he swallowed and breathed excitely.

- "Soulqam! You are alive! Are you okay?" Aridem shouted and ran to meet his friend.

Soulqam, who said "I'm fine, I'm fine..." slowed down the run and came to Aridem and started to catch her breathe again.

- "I thought you were dead..." Said Aridem with sadness in his eyes and gave a hug to his friend.

Accepting the hug, Soulqam said, "So am I." and she saw the feeling of guilt in Aridem's eyes and continued: "You have no crime; you have done well with fleeing. There was nothing you could do!"

- "I am sorry… I thought you were all dead… But how? What happened?" Aridem asked uneasily.

- "I will tell you; I will tell you all." Answered Soulqam, gathered at the head of the guards and greeted them and spent a little more time to catch her breath.

Soulqam, thinking that she had to make a statement as soon as possible in confused and curious glances looked at Aridem one last time and began to shake her head.

She shouted, "Oh dear community!" She thought the word "Community" that she just used and felt that later this word could be perceived as disdain, she corrected her address as "Oh dear guards!" and when she saw that Aridem was smirking as he reassured her of her confidence, so she told every detail of the events to the crowd what was happened with Blaad and the terms of the agreement one by one. The negative and positive attitudes of the crowd showed that they did not trust Blaad. Moreover, saying that Soulqam was talking about the king and the queen, and that they were in rottenness in the dungeon brought all the people to wrath.

The fact that no one was acting discreetly and talking about their attack plans from the very first minute spooked Aridem. "Listen to Soulqam! It might be a good deal!" He yelled at the crowd, but the effort was futile.

The guards, who were already eager to attack, started shouting all together: "Let's attack without losing any time!" And these screams turned into a verse.

- "Aridem, they will go to their deaths, please stop them!" Soulqam approached Aridem and watched the crowd in a terrified manner.

- "Maybe they have a chance?" Aridem asked.

- "Never!" Soulqam shouted without thinking and said: "You do not know what I have seen. They cannot even have a little bit chance! He has magic, and he is too strong!"

- "All right... But there's no way we can stop them. Do you not see that they are very keen and ready to attack? But if you say so, then I will stay here with you. As I trust you…" Said Aridem and it made Soulqam calmed a bit down.

The guards started marching out with noises and cheers.

"They are going to their deaths, they are all going to die..." Whispered Soulqam, sadly speaking, saw nothing but the guards going through her sad eyes...

The Massacre

The castle was shaken by the base of it which made Blaad lost his concentration while watching the portrait of his love, recognizing that something big hit the wall of the castle, Blaad wore the waist with the curved dagger standing at the table and headed out.

While he was approaching to the main door, he heard another big noise, and the castle was shaken again.

Aypher, shouting "My lord!", transformed himself in the form of werewolf and was ready to go out.

Blaad lifted his hand up, saying, "They are attacking to our castle..." and continued, "No, you are not going out! I will handle this alone!"

The frustration on Aypher's face, "Why?" was evident even in the werewolf form.

- "You will keep your distance, and you won't let anybody to enter the castle!" Commanded Blaad and continued: "Besides, you do not know when to stop..."

Blaad meant no offence against his last sentence, but Aypher was disappointed and opted to remain silent and turned his head back to the large saloon.

Blaad, who opened the castle door with a magic word, casted himself a magic spell and formed an invisible shield that surrounds him.

"So, you chose to attack me instead of finding Haipe!" Roared Blaad, stepping out of the castle despite the painful rays of the sun.

By seeing the two ballistas that were targeting the castle, he was distracted for a second and understood the cause of the damage. The first spell he made was to create two large fireballs, and he sent these fireballs over the ballistas. The ballistas fell apart by the falling of the fireballs on them, and they started to burn by crackling.

Seeing a dozen of horsemen who began to run towards him, Blaad turned his hands onto them and began to say another word of magic. A big lightning bolt or a big fireball could turn all of them into ashes, but Blaad did not want to hurt the horses, thinking of another spell and starting to move his hands forward.

Dozens of acid arrows formed in front of Blaad and hung up in the air while waiting for orders. Blaad closed his eyes and hold up until the guards were close enough in range. Waiting for the guards to get closer to the castle, Blaad opened his eyes and gave orders to the arrows. Arrows dripping acids from the tips were thrown forward and stuck in the throats of the guards, making them all falling over the horses.

The guards tried to hold and grasp the wreckage of their broken and burning throats, but it was too late, and they began to die in turn, without even being able to make a scream.

The mass deaths of the guards gave immediate sorrow to the swordsmen unity that were coming from behind. The swordsmen raised their shields to their fronts and entered the formation to reminisce a rectangle, and slowly began to walk towards the hill.

Watching the shameful defence format in front of him, Blaad smiled and started to rise in the air by opening his hands. Blaad, who thought he had risen enough, went forward, hung himself up to the tops of the swordsmen, and began to cast his spell.

Those who had spears from the swordsmen threw their spears into the air, but even some of the spears did reach their target, they have thrown back by the magic shield that was surrounding Blaad and fell to the ground without doing any damage.

With the voice of a master swordsman shouting, "The shields to the air!" all the shields faced the air, but it was so clear that the shields could not provide protection against lightning from the hands of Blaad, who formed and released the spell.

Lightning struck the swordsmen's feet on the ground, and the swordsmen were killed before they could fall. Although the inanimate bodies on the ground encounter the earth, they continue to tremble and shake for a long time due to the heavily charged electricity.

The last survived guards regiment began to retreat and escape towards the forest when they realized they were desperate in the face of the sightings, but Blaad, who was blurring his eyes, came down and followed the guards that were trying to run away.

The armour voices of the guards who flee into and out of the forest were powerful enough to awaken a half-deaf man from his sleep. Therefore, Blaad, having no difficulty in locating the position of guards, continued marching towards to the village by killing the guards against him with various spells. He enjoyed the variety of spells that he has been using and collected enough blood supply into his dagger.

The red dagger "RedBlaad" in his belt was glowing immensely because of the bloodshed which Blaad found out a while ago that the dagger's ability was holding a massive amount of blood in it and keeping it fresh in case he needs it. The amount he collected would be enough for him for a year or so.

Blaad, confident that no living guards were left around the forest, put himself in the form of a mist and, for the first time, turned himself into a wolf. He pressed on the ground with his hands and feet and realized that his eyes were sharpened, and quickly examined his new body, "Aypher should see this..." He spoke while smirking, and with the full speed began to run towards to the village.

Blaad never stopped until he reached the village, and when he realized that he had come to the entrance of the village, he took the mist form and turned himself back into his human form.

He caught sight of a man looking at him with surprise and attacked his neck and drank his blood. The burns that were formed in the body due to the exposure of sunlight were immediately healed and regenerated. In a few minutes, the unlucky person whose blood was sucked from his body, fell over near the feet of Blaad.

Blaad, whose powers have been restored, has renewed his magical shield, and waited, letting the crowd gathered around him in the circle.

- "I told you to find Haipe, but you chose to attack me!" Blaad yelled at the crowd.

- "We do not have your Haipe!" A voice came from the crowd.

Another voice was heard: "You hold our king and our queen as prisoners!"

- "You killed the guards!" Another man shouted.

- "But you will die too! For our king and our queen!" A guard shouted and thrown forward and started the attack.

Blaad, who said, "Oh, hell to your king and your queen!" instead of attacking the crowd that coming closer, chose to disperse in the air by taking the mist form.

The crowd in the environment began to hurt each other and when they realized that the vampire was lost, then they stopped and began to look around with fear in the presence of screams and shouts.

Blaad, who took the human form a little beyond the crowd, watched the crowd crushing each other with pleasure and casted a powerful conjuring magic spell by reaching out his hands to the front. There was a slit on the ground with a small shake where he sent the magic, and the sword spiders that came out of the slit began attacking people with Blaad's telepathic orders.

Standing on his back, Blaad watched the battle in front of him and caught people trying to escape with his spiders by giving orders, not even leaving one of them alive. When he was sure no one was alive from the crowd, he sent his spider away to where they came from, and he was surprised by the massacre that he had done in a short time. A sword spider was one of a kind and very powerful creature especially comparing with unorganised peasants and there were a few of them around that he summoned. "Maybe I am the one who does not know when to stop." Blaad realized that he was unfair to his friend Aypher.

Later, he concentrated on his eyes that were in a special mode that senses heat and ultra-vision. He scanned the surroundings and identified two people hiding in a small house.

He brought himself to the mist form and then took the bat form and quickly entered the house from the window and took the human form again.

- "Soulqam! Aridem!" Blaad looked angrily at his old friends.

- "No!" Soulqam screamed.

- "Don't do it, we are not guilty!" Aridem shouted and began to explain, "Those who did not listen to us did this, they prefer to attack!"

Blaad shouted, "Shut up!" and casted a spell to Aridem and temporarily paralyzed him.

Soulqam shouted: "He is telling the truth; they have not listened to us!" It was now difficult to stand up for her, maybe feeling the last minutes of her life.

- "We had a deal..." Blaad lowered his voice and walked over, looking into Soulqam's eye.

- "Please..." Begged Soulqam in a last effort, but Blaad's hand was already on Soulqam's thin neck.

The grasping hand pulled Soulqam toward him and he began to suck her blood, biting with his vampire teeth into her delicate neck. Soulqam did not have the strength to resist this time. She could only look at Aridem and spoke silently to him: "I… Love… You…"

Leaving Soulqam's lifeless body slightly out of the way, Blaad took Aridem whose face was full of tears on to his arms while he was in his paralyzed position on the floor and kicked the door of the house. For one last moment, Blaad stopped and viewed the massacre that he has done and once again looked at it and began to walk towards to his castle with quick steps while carrying Aridem on his shoulders. He just eradicated a whole village from the map, and he was not sure how to feel about that…

The Blood Algae

- "You're sure we're on the right track, aren't you?" Zegan asked while cleaning his boots and started looking at his friends.

- "That's what the map says." Monem replied politely.

- "Why was this dirtiest duty given to us?" Complained Doan, who was struggling to keep the balance in order to avoid the accumulation of sludgy and mushy ground in front of him.

Monem said, "We're almost there, we're about to come." pointing to the big bog in front of them.

- "Now I will not be surprised if some swamp monsters come out!" Zegan laughed and pulled his sword, he was joking but still he really wouldn't have surprised if something had come out of the mud!

- Doan, who said, "Oh, I cannot do more nastiness." put his hand on to his sword and grasped it very tight.

- "According to the map, there will be a small statue on the edge of the marsh, and we will find the blood algae there." Spoke Monem.

Zegan and Doan, "Good, good." who speak the same phrase at the same time, laughed.

The trio approached the marsh with the sounds of their armour, and they came before the statue Monem mentioned. The marvellous statue resembled a mermaid and the magnificent beauty on the face of the statue was fascinating.

Doan, saying, "I would give my everything if it was to be real..." couldn't blink his eyes for a second.

- "Like you said..." Whispered Zegan and touched on the smooth surface of the statue with his hands.

- "Friends, leave the statue alone now..." Even Monem made a glimpse to the statue.

- "No, we won't!" Joked Zegan and Doan at the same time again.

- "Seriously…" Monem rolled his eyes.

- "So, what is so special about the statue and why is it on the map?" Asked Zegan, eyes were still on the statue, without blinking.

- "I really want to know too, hmm, Monem, can you cast stone to flesh spell please on it?" Doan was not joking this time.

- "Really? Do you think it was real and turned to stone somehow?" Asked Monem, thinking about if he can really cast a powerful spell like that.

- "It could be, let's try and find out?" Suggested Doan.

- "Yes, please do it Monem!" Zegan was also feeling excited with the thought of the statue coming back alive.

Monem pausd for a second, thought of trying to cast a spell like that, but then stopped and asked to the duo: "So, let's say, I managed to do the spell, turned it back to flesh, and then what? Who is going to be her saviour? I mean do you think you have a chance; you know what I mean…"

- "Of course, she would choose me over you guys!" Giggled Doan and then looked at Zegan.

- "No, of course I will be the one!" Laughed Zegan but thought about what would have happened if she really could come to life.

- "Looks like we got competition!" Smiled Monem while looking at them. He had no intention of doing that magic; but he added: "She will be the one who does the choice guys!" Then he saw that they are not listening but watching the statue with their mouths open. Monem smiled again and shook his head.

Perhaps the only thing that brought the group that watched the statue for some minute was the swelling and movement of the water. Three heads came out of the swamp and the unnaturally charming bodies approaching them began to ascend from the water.

Doan cut off his breath, saying, "It is real…", stepping forward, unable to stand on the unavoidable gaze of the three mermaids from the swamp.

- "But how?" gasped Zegan, who asked himself this question, answered the unavoidable gaze of the mermaid in front of him, and began to walk with his hands on his front resembling a zombie.

- "No, wait, don't…" Spoke Monem, who was not able to turn his face against the sea and the mermaids, and his inner voice was saying that they were going into a very wrong way.

The mermaids, despite the mud of the marsh, had come out of the swamp in pristine condition, and the sun rays reflected on their thin transparent clothes on their bodies which made them look even prettier. The mermaids who started touching the warriors with their delicate touches, blinked at them, smiled and enchanted.

Doan became unable to feel even that he was alive and began to enter the marsh with the mermaid in a state of completely being charmed.

Zegan did not need any charming spell or even an invite, he lost consciousness by the image of the mermaid as she touched his arms and his hairs, and smiled like a drunk, and happily walked with the mermaid into the marsh.

The other mermaid, whispering to Monem's ear with her wet mouth, "Come with me..." while Monem was trying to keep his discipline and resisting the charm, held Monem's hands with her hands and began to pull.

Monem was perhaps having the most unrelenting battle of his life, and the only thing that drove Monem to recover himself was the sight of blood algae which attached to his foot. He remembered where he was and the significance of his task with the purpose, and he pushed the mermaid hard, readying his sword.

Monem, angered the mermaid, looked at his friends for a moment and saw that they had entered the marsh as far as their half of the bodies and they were not stopping! "No! Stop!" Monem yelled, but as the appearances of his friends, he understood they did not hear himself. Without losing time, he casted a protection from evil spell to cover himself and his friends.

With the influence of protection spell, the enchantment that covered the mermaids were disappeared and their true faces and images appeared. All the disgusting faces were there to see, and the mermaids, aware of the fake images were off on them, began to fascinate an evil spell with their long-fingered dirty hands.

Recognizing that an evil magic was about to be casted, Monem immediately casted another magic shield and managed to hold his friends in the arms of the shore.

The chants of the mermaids were completed, and they sent it to the trio with a green light; but the green spell was crushed by the magic shield that Monem created and destroyed both the evil spell and the magic shield itself.

"They pierced my magic shield! They can cast powerful spells! Get ready! To arms!" Monem shouted, warning his friends, and starting another identifier magic. If he could identify what they were against at, he would think of an advantage of overcoming the challenge. After casting his quick spell, Monem yelled: "These are sea nymphs! Evil sea nymphs! Or evil sea witches!"

"Just tell me how to kill them!" Was the very reasonable question of Doan. The lack of a response from Monem moved Doan into action and he was thrown forward with his sword to take revenge for the incredible deceiver he got by the nymphs' buff. Doan definitely believed that he would bring a blow to the nymph in front, but he gave all his strength to his sword, but when the nymph was disappeared and it appeared behind, he lost his balance and buried his face in the mud of the marsh, cursing while puking mud out of his mouth.

Zegan attacked to rescue his friend and ran the short distance in front of him and tried to hit the nymph by cutting from right to left with his sword. The nymph disappeared in the same way, concealing the attack of the blade, and the nymph that appeared at a distance close to Monem started to laugh with her yellow rotten teeth. However, the smile of the nymph ended as soon as she realized that she was immobile. She could not even close her eyes because of the magic that covered the nymph and broke her curved snout that hit the centre of her face, killing her by the nose bone into her brain before she even made a small sound.

As their sisters died, the nymphs began to run to Monem, screaming, and they disappeared again to pass Doan and Zegan, who were standing still with their swords, covered with mud. The nymphs had already taken one or two steps to their final approach to their target. But Doan and Zegan were ready, and they saw the nymphs' tactics once, so they dug their swords towards their backs, and crushed the nymphs from their backs, killing them at the same time as the swords coming out of their bellies. The last image of the eyes of the nymphs was the divine face of Monem. It was such a great tactics that they have been training on for some time and they were both proud of it.

Doan, who said, "We did it!" sank with his hands on the mud and spat on the nymph he had killed.

- "It was fine but disgusting... But was also very funny!" Zegan laughed with his friends.

- "You were both very enchanted by the very simple charming spell! A bit more discipline!" Monem, who raised his voice, was obviously not enjoying the conversation. He couldn't imagine what would have happened if he hadn't resisted the spell.

The couple, who witnessed rare moments when Monem was angry, quieted, and watched Monem gather the blood algae from the floor without saying anything.

Thinking that he was collecting enough blood algae briefly, Monem pulled the bundle in his armour's pocket, poured the blood algae into the bundle, and knotted the cohort and left it on the floor.

As soon as the bundle was left on the floor, which started to fly by shaking the mud on it, disappeared into the sky, Monem had already begun to return...

The Tundra Mushroom

Dhammal, thinking that he did not need his map anymore, confirmed the last time he was in the desired place and proceeded with cautious steps toward the entrance of the cave and left the wind with his strong grasps.

Against the coldness of the air, he cursed once again for not wearing any armour and ran into the cavern without thinking where he felt the warm air flow, which was enough to complete his task without freezing. The vigorous air contrasting with the outside reduced the vibrations and shrivelled up the snow on them.

Taking a few more steps, Dhammal finally realized that his foot was touching a trap, but without pulling his leg, he flew head-on into the air and began to swing from his foot to his back. He cursed again because of his carelessness, but when he saw a figure coming out of the shadows and approaching towards him, he stood still in his position, up in the air, trying to hold his balance even he was upside down.

Dhammal, who looked at the figure with his eyes narrowed, thought that she was a female orc first, but she also looked very human, so he was hesitant and did not know how to react but said: "Uhm, hello."

- "Give me a reason not to kill you!" Said the half-orc, pulling her spear out of her back and putting it on Dhammal's neck.

- "Mushroom! Tundra mushroom!" Said Dhammal suddenly.

- "Hah!" The half-orc said with a short laugh but with a squeaky punch, and said, "Your last chance, tell me the truth now!"

- "I am telling the truth! I'll just collect some mushrooms and I'll go back on my way very quickly! Whoever is with you or whatever you are after will not be touched!" Dhammal made a statement, saying, "For your own sake, let me be on my way!" He took a deep breath when he felt that the spear was slightly away from his throat.

- "Actually, I can use you..." Thought the half-orc who began to vocalize and began to examine Dhammal's muscular body.

- "Use me? Okay, whatever you want, I can help you with." Said Dhammal and realized that he could cut himself down on to the half-orc if he could draw her attention in some other direction.

- "The white dragon..." Said the half-orc, with a narrow cry, and continued: "Kill the white dragon, and I will let you go."

- "Ha-ha!" The line of laughing was now on Dhammal. He laughed and continued to laugh, saying, "There couldn't be dragons, oh no, there are no dragons! Oh, are there? Are you serious?"

- "Then you will need good luck, hopefully some mushroom or not, if you can stay alive." The half-orc who bluffed, put her spear on her back and turned back to Dhammal.

Right at that moment Dhammal, lying on his feet, clung to a halter, and cut off the ropes without any difficulty and turned over in the air and landed on his feet. He took a big step forward and nodded with the half-orc, handling, and turning toward her and pulling her towards to himself. The half-orc, whose fingers remained on their side and could not move, began to look at Dhammal with her eyes opened horrified. Dhammal gave her a big smile and released the half-orc free, feeling the orchestrated heartbeats in her chest.

Dhammal, who gave his hand to his new friend and said, "Let's kill your dragon together, what do you think?" Thought that he would act the same if he was the half-orc.

The half-orc, who answered "Well... Okay." swallowed hard a few times to make herself calm, but she did not separate her eyes from Dhammal.

- "Come on then." Dhammal said, putting his hands on his belly and pointing the way with his eyes, he made a half-hearted smile and began to walk into the cave. In fact, he was very happy to see someone to talk to, especially a female one, orc or human, it didn't matter, after many years of spending his days with his buddies.

- "I'm coming! Wait for me!" The half-orc said, recovering her courage by feeling that she was impressed by Dhammal's trusting look.

Walking together for a few minutes, a giant hall opened in front of the mouth of the cave, and they began to look at each other.

- "The dragon is there." Whispered the half-orc.

- "I can guess." Dhammal said with a sneaky look.

- "What's your plan?" She asked.

- "To go in and attack." Dhammal replied very comfortably.

- "A great plan..." Said the half-orc, looking at the direction they came from as for a moment she regretted coming together, and thought it was too late to return.

- "Why do you want it dead? Why do we kill the dragon, you tell me first." Dhammal said, causing the half-orc to turn towards him again.

- "Because it is evil, it killed my tribe, and it does not give any chance for any other tribes to live!" Said the half-orc.

- "Revenge..." Said Dhammal.

- "Yes!" Confirmed the half-orc.

- "Can I ask you something?" Dhammal said, causing half-orc angry.

- "Ask!" Said the half-orc with exhaustion.

- "Is it true that you came from the elves?" Dhammal asked.

- "What the hell are you talking about?" Said the half-orc, and thought of attacking Dhammal for a second, not to the dragon.

- "I heard it from somewhere, I wanted to learn, do not worry about it, do not worry." Dhammal pointed out that it was silent and made himself even more annoying by the eyes of the half-orc.

- "You are talking non-sense! Why do you ask such question, are you mocking me? Are you trying to make me angry? I hate elves!" Said half-orc, but Dhammal did not listen.

Dhammal entered the giant hall of the cave with as silent as possible and was breathless when he saw the enormous beauty of the massive dragon sleeping in the middle of the hall. The white prints of the dragon looked alike, and with the cold air from its deep breaths, the scales instantly changing into rainbow colours.

Dhammal, who watched the dragon for a long time, was anxious for a moment when he noticed the approaching half-orc but could not lift his eyes from the harmony of the dragon's colour changing scales.

The half-orc, who started saying, "Go on, go and attack, like you say so." teased Dhammal.

- "Wait a minute… It is such a beauty…" Dhammal paused, looks fascinated.

- "A beauty? It is pure evil! It is everything but beauty!" Angrily spoke half-orc.

- "I know, I know…" Shushed Dhammal.

- "Tundra mushrooms, look at them..." The half-orc said, pointing to the side walls next to Dhammal.

Dhammal, seeing the mushrooms, cut off a pinch of them from the wall quickly if it was a negative scenario, then took the empty bundle hanging from the belt and filled the mushrooms into it. Dhammal responded to the half-orc with a smile to her unobservable gaze and squeezed the mouth of the bundle and left it onto the ground. The half-orcs eyes widened as the bundle flew back and forth away from the cave and disappeared from her eyes and turned to Dhammal and asked with a small shock: "You are a sorcerer, aren't you?"

Dhammal's smile grew, and he said, "No, I am a barbarian, I don't have magic; but I have a sorcerer friend, and he's a lich." The half-orc stunned that could not conceal her astonishment after all the strangeness that she had already experienced; but Dhammal reminded of the seriousness of the situation, saying, "Let's observe the creature cautiously, and prepare for an attack." and the faces of the two of them turned back to the dragon again.

Listening to everything spoken, the dragon stopped its fake sleep and opened its eyes. It stared at them without disturbing and looked at Dhammal and asked: "Mushrooms?"

At that moment, there was such a wave of fear that both knees began to tremble, and they both thought of cuddling and hugging each other like children. Dhammal was the first to succeed in defeating through fear and shook the half-orc he had wrapped up, allowing her to be at herself again.

Dhammal, who said, "Yes... Mushrooms... Oh great dragon..." thinking how helpless he is in front of the giant dragon.

The half-orc who managed to say "What are you doing..." did not stop Dhammal by saying things like that.

- "Shut up and learn how to talk with dragons." Dhammal said quietly and turned to the dragon and continued: "Oh the glorious dragon, we have heard your glory and we came up from the surface for these beautiful mushrooms that your unique breath raised. Let us have some of the mushrooms, oh wise and great dragon!"

- "Stupid!" Whispered half-orc, thinking surely, they were both going to die.

Dhammal's condemnation, which started again as "Oh the greatest dragon of all...", was cut in the half with the dragon's head lifted.

"You idiots!" Yelled the dragon first, and roared, "Do you think I have not heard your conversations since the beginning?"

Dhammal, aware of the icicles hanging from the ceiling of the cave by the dragon's head, weighed on whether he could kill the dragon if he could break the stalactite with a hit by throwing his hammer, but he gave up this idea, thinking that it would be a real risk to remain unarmed.

- "So, you heard everything." Dhammal said, developing another method: "Did you also hear that I am a friend of the lich? And that the lich is waiting for me outside of the cave? And the thousands of orcs are ready to attack at any moment for your treasury?"

The tone of the dragon, saying, "Is the lich here?" showed that it had eaten the bluff.

- "What do you think? Even at this exact moment, he is there, on your back!" Dhammal said confidently and when the dragon got confused and started turning its head behind, he really threw his war hammer to the icicles on the head of the dragon.

The glacier stalactite, just like Dhammal thinks, was hit by the war hammer, and fell on the dragon's neck. Dhammal, however, watched with disappointment that the icicles had fallen on the ground without damaging the dragon and didn't even scratch the neck of its scales, saying: "Damn! What was I thinking? Now I am unarmed!" But he suddenly made his decision and grabbed the half-orc's spear, began to run with a war cry, and jumped on to the dragon, holding the spear very tight with his hands.

When the dragon felt something on itself and an object slid down to the neck of the top and realized Dhammal's face, it turned to its forehead again. The dragon was about to open its mouth and send an ice-cone, but the long and the rusty spear that pierced into its eye caused it a painful scream. The dragon lifted its head and started to whine like crazy despite its badly hurt eyes, but this caused more pain as Dhammal hurt him more because he did not leave the spear and no matter how hard it tried, Dhammal was holding the spear without leaving his grip on it.

Dhammal realized that he was enjoying the dragon's swings and began to laugh at the madness he had made. Feeling that the dragon had lowered his head down, Dhammal pulled the spear out of the eye and protected the balance and stuck it in the other eye, lifting the dragon head fully.

The dragon, completely blind, shouted with anger and opened his mouth and began spraying ice-cones around him. It just wanted to get rid of the human on it so it could get away and heal itself as the critical hits were not something it calculated.

Dhammal, aware of the cold air blowing from the feet of his leg, grasped all the power. He knew that when the cold air encountered him, he would become completely ice. Dhammal suddenly thrust his spear deeply, throwing a serious push and nail. Having heard a crackling, Dhammal realized that the tip of the spear had knocked on the dragon's skull, and with a final effort he pushed his spear a little more. The outside part of the spear was almost a difficult one to hold, but with his strong hands, Dhammal pushed the spear into the white dragon's brain and caused the dragon to fall and die instantly... The spear was now unseen and completely inside of the dragon.

Leaving himself on the dragon's scales to which he had just killed, Dhammal rested for a short while and called the half-orc by his side, who was watching him shockingly in her place. Half-orc came to her hero without complaining and walked on the dragon and sat next to Dhammal.

- "You did as you said... You came in and attacked... And you killed the beast! Wow! You are really, really very, very strong!" Said the half-orc, looking at Dhammal and lying beside him with admiration.

- "I am. It was direct and uninterrupted! And sorry about your spear, I don't think you would want it back, yuck!" Dhammal replied with joke and pleasure and moved his hands over the white dragon's scales, which he had slaughtered with his hands as well.

- "I have not seen that much strength before." Said the half-orc, continuing to sift through Dhammal and his muscles, "And my vengeance is over now."

- "Yes... That's great, isn't it? But I must go now..." Dhammal took a deep breath and started to say, "I finished my job, your tribe is free, and now my friends..."

- "Don't go!" Said the half-orc, pushing Dhammal through his chest with her hands as an obstacle to Dhammal's culmination, and said, "Spend the night here and you may leave in the morning."

- "But..." Dhammal spoke and understood that he could not appeal and leave her there. Meanwhile the half-orc, who came closer to him, ran her eyes over his body.

The half-orc whispered, "Spend the night with me...", despite the chill, she took the thick platter on herself and jumped over Dhammal. Dhammal, who realized that he was in such a position that he couldn't resist, he just wanted to say no for a second but then let go, and released his muscles and handed himself over to the semi-dressed half-orc who had already taken over control...

Soon after they left, a hooded figure appeared from nowhere right at the entrance of the cave and walked inside without any noise... Blaad, who took his red dagger from his belt, started casting a dark complicated spell over the dead body of the dragon and spread some blood from his dagger. A few seconds later, the reanimated dragon started moving his dead body and opened its blind eyes. The eyes were looking at nothingness, empty and blurry but also creepy. "Fly now to the chateau and destroy everything you find!" Ordered Blaad to the undead dragon and walked outside without looking back... This had been their game between Blaad and Behim since the beginning; they were sending monsters or creatures to each other just for fun and they knew nothing would ever defeat them, but they kept doing this for no reason. But this time Blaad was expecting that the undead dragon would be a real headache for Behim... The evil smile on Blaad's pale face was stupendous...

The Paladin and The Barbarian

"I guess that would be all, my friends! It was an honour to fight alongside with you..." Monem shouted and tore the head off the orc against him with his powerful long sword. His arms and legs were not restrained, he murmured a short hymn once more to make himself a weary spell. Slowly clinging to the sword with divine energy spreading to his body, Monem smiled, staring at the pile of the corpses of the orcs that were gathered around him. He saw another tricky orc who was trying to approach from his left side with bloodlust, but quickly raised his shield to neutralize the orc's attack with the shield that he had fixed to his left side and completed his movement by piercing orc's bowels by his long sword and cleaned the blood on his face to look at his friends.

The trust in their friends with whom they set out together was endless. They also trusted Monem, and they regarded him as a Paladin as their leader. They had never left each other in any circumstances, but this time they were not paying enough attention as this ambush was unbelievable for them. It looked like the orcs appeared from nowhere!

Monem, cleaning up the blood on his face again, looked at Doan and Zegan, and sadly understood that they could not keep up, and they knew that no matter how great they were fighting, they would not be able to stand the last of the fight. Zegan's left leg was injured by a deep spear impact, and his right eye was swollen and closed with blood. It was a matter of time for both of them to fall.

"Fighting with honour and dying with it..." Monem thought once again, and he prepared another divine spell for himself for a last strike. He had the last hymn he had hid for his glorious deaths, and it was the right time to do it. Monem's concentration, touching his hands against each other, began to cast the powerful divine magic, was fizzled when he realized a piercing long spear on the back of Doan. Doan fell to his right side by hand and took his other hand to his arm and looked desperately at Monem. Doan, who was bleeding from his mouth by coughing, could not breathe because his lungs were punctured. Doan, who opened his eyes with a last effort, tried to place a smile on his face, but it was too late. The deadly stroke made by another orc's axe cracked his skull and caused Doan to die.

Zegan hesitated for a moment, following the disastrous death of his friend, who just fell in front of his feet. He grinned at the head of his friend and responded with ranting, and from such a stalled falcon he rose from such a position that he had to pierce his enemies several times in order to reach the grimmer of the laughing orc. Zegan wiped his crying eyes and touched Doan's head, closing his eyes, and standing here for a short while. Zegan's breathed very hardly as he had gathered the air to his lungs for the last time. Zegan lifted his head, staring at Monem, and began to run wildly towards the mass of orcs across, suiciding himself.

Monem's "No! Don't!" cries were drowning under the laughter of the orcs. He hammered the centre of his shield with his fist and yelled "Come on then!" to the orcs in front of him and struck them in the torso with a shield and dropped a few of them down, and he found a bitter taste in his mouth and dropped another orc from the heap.

Zegan dashed through the orcs that were now virtually invisible to him. Acting only instinctively, Zegan did not feel his injured stomach. He noticed a strike coming from his left, but his legs were inconvenient for this sudden movement. His leg was twisted, and he found himself on the ground. The axe standing against him lifted on his face towards him and instead of a fear, he began to smile by thinking about his fate. Then he turned his face to his right arm and looked at the wristband and said with a raucous voice, "Ouzan, forgive me my brother, I couldn't make it..." Zegan realized that the orc had raised his battle axe in the air, but did not feel the blow to his head.

After the fall of Zegan, all the vicious orcs turned their ugly faces to Monem. Looking at the stack in front, Monem, who calculated from his mind, counted perhaps as close to 200 orcs. Where were they coming from and where they have been living or hiding, the thoughts were not very important, but Monem was full of various questions. The orcs were afraid of Monem because of the fact that there was a very strong Paladin fighting to them, and this situation was holding some of the orcs, but there was not much that Monem could do against these undeniable odds.

Accepting death, Monem once again looked at his shield and his long sword and sparked them once again by hitting them each other. Then he lifted his sword to his chest and mumbled another hymn. The light beam from the sky spread to his sword and to his shield, bringing them into an eye-catching brightness.

Monem began to take small but cautious steps toward the orcs, then started smiling which spreads across his face, when he heard a war cry that resembled the roar of a bear over the opposite hill. Perhaps all of the orcs turned their backs against this war cry and saw a figure resembling a giant standing on the top of the hill with an enormous size of a war hammer in his hands.

The giant figure, shouting another war cry, started his departure from the top to the orcs running around in delicacy, caused Monem's mouth to open up to his ears because of the cheer. He knew the giant figure that came, was his old friend Dhammal the barbarian!

The first group of orcs that came across by Dhammal, with such a stunning war hammer, hurled so much that orcs were blown up by a lightning strike. Dhammal, who had devastated at least five orcs in each swing of the war hammer, slowly began to reach Monem.

Monem's morale boost came to power, and he proceeded confidently through the eyes toward the panicked orcs. Orcs that do not already have any gear to block such attacks have escaped to the left and right and started to hit each other in panic.

Although Dhammal's and Monem's fighting styles were very different from each other, these differences enabled the orcs to lose their discipline even further. Dhammal was directly attacking his opponent in front of him, accepting the hits from the enemy, even though he was not wearing any armour, and he was moving like a berserker. Monem draws circles with his dazzling armour and shield and attacks his rival from the front or side with his decisive technique.

Monem killed most of the orcs in front of him quickly, and when he was sure that he did not have any orcs around him, he set his feet on the ground and watched Dhammal. He then waved his hand to Dhammal and mumbled a quick hymn and sent an empowering spell to Dhammal.

Recognizing that his arms and legs grew even more, Dhammal laughed at Monem and shouted, "I do not need it, but thanks anyway!"

With Dhammal's involvement in the fight, the war, which was about to be lost, changed to other side. The orcs did not want to face with Dhammal, but Dhammal ran from behind them, caught them, and fought them with his deadly blows. For those who were less lucky to approach him had the worst fate as he struck them down from above with his war hammer and crushed their heads.

As he tried to kill a runner orc that survived a swing of him, threw his war hammer to the back of the orc. Then two orcs, who saw Dhammal to be unarmed, tried to attack Dhammal, but Dhammal's muscular arms like pincers caught the orcs heads and caused them to hit each other suddenly and die.

Dhammal saw Monem, who was watching and admiring him, and responded to Monem's smile. As the orcs screamed and disappeared from sight, he grabbed and hung the war hammer on his back and walked toward Monem.

- "Just in time, old friend…" Spoke Monem, putting his long sword near his belt and greeting Dhammal with his shield while putting it on his back.

- "It looks like that!" Replied Dhammal.

- "How did you know we were here?" Asked Monem, giving his hand to Dhammal.

- "We were using the same path, and I heard the screams of orcs." Dhammal replied, reached out his hand to Monem and shook hands with Monem's grim look. After the shake, they hugged each other strongly and firmly.

- "How did you fall into such a trap?" Asked Dhammal and Monem clutched over into silence.

- "No, it was not a trap... They knew we were going to the great meeting... Orcs are not smart enough to make such plans." Said Monem, showing the dead orcs.

- "Oh, could it be him?" Dhammal opened his eyes like a fortune teller.

- "Yes, I first thought it was an ordinary association of orcs, but it was not. And yes, it is surely him..." Monem approved.

- "Are we late for the meeting?" Dhammal asked.

- "We will be there on time, if we leave immediately, but there are some things to do..." Monem changed his face's direction to his dead friends.

Dhammal asked, "What happened?" and he turned his eyes toward the battlefield, analysing the environment.

- "Zegan and Doan... There was nothing I could do..." Quietly answered Monem.

Monem's silent reply caused Dhammal, who had a hard look, to fall into a big sorrow. He went after Monem, who was moving towards the battlefield, and first realized Doan's and then Zegan's lifeless bodies. There was a "Doan..." whisper in his mouth, but he could not even hear it himself.

Both put the inanimate bodies side by side as they dragged towards the tree standing in front of them and laid them on their backs. Dhammal recovered and allowed Monem to rest for a while, without losing any time, immediately by digging the ground.

Before burying the bodies, Monem took Zegan's wristband from his arm and put it on his own arm. To Dhammal's questioning glances, he replied, "You know his brother gave it to him, but I still do not know why, but it was very valuable to him." and kissed their foreheads one last time and thanked them for their braveries with whispers.

Covering the dead bodies with a clean shirt, Monem smoothed the grave with his hand, and began to chisel it by putting the large rock brought by Dhammal near to the head of the grave. He wrote exactly on the rock:

"Here lies Zegan and Doan.

They fought with honour.

Died with honour.

May 18, 2016 "

Monem's chronicle of 2016 caught Dhammal's attention and asked to him: "Are you still following the old calendar? The concept of time here seems to work a bit differently, and I think there is no year 2016 here." Monem's answer was just a shoulder shrug.

After finishing his work, Monem accepted the help of Dhammal's strong hand and stood on his feet and shrugged the dust off his cloak and looked toward the path in front of them.

- "Should we continue on the road? Or would you like to rest?" Dhammal asked.

- "I do not want to waste any more time." Answered Monem.

They started to walk together. Monem turned his back to the battlefield and checked the graves of his lost friends for the last time. "This happened because of you Blaad, always because of you..." Spoke Monem by squeezing his fists and they continued their way...

The Rogue

For the last time, the sleepless rogue, U, checked his backpack again and headed to the door to say goodbye to his little shed where he kept hiding for some time.

He usually preferred to travel in the darkest time of night, because he was like the night itself; quiet and deadly.

He was about to raise his hand to open the door, he heard a crackling sound coming from outside and quickly stepped back. He murmured, "Still not enough?" and immediately hid himself in the shadows and began to hold on his breath.

The door opened without squeaking, and the man who had walked in took a blade out of his pocket without hesitating and headed for the bed in the corner. The man who lifted his blade was not aware that the bed was empty, but he noticed the edge of two daggers coming out of his heart.

The man who was trying to cover his chest with his empty hand turned around and met U with his dark and bitter look. " Still not enough?" He said to the man, holding the man's hand holding the knife and turning it, and cut the man's throat with the knife. U threw the man with a kick and passed the hood over his head and took the backpack on the floor and headed for the door again.

After opening the door, he looked at the shed he had stayed in for the last time and went out and had a little look again to say goodbye to his shed. He knew it was the last time seeing his small shed.

He had taken a few steps to realize that there were two mischievous fools hiding in the sides of the tree opposite his shed and he turned to the back of the bandits in quick but silent steps. The men had never even noticed that U was behind them, and both were watching the shed in an uneasy situation. Most likely they were expecting their friends to complete their dirty work and return to their side.

They scolded with a "Boo!" from U and could not choose the eyes of the men who were turning their backs, and at the same time, they had a dagger stuck in their eyes and they both died on the spot without understanding what it was. The stabbing movement of U was a pencil-like withdrawn at the same speed and the daggers reverted to the arches of the waist belt.

'Still not enough?" He examined the environment, and then turned his head toward the bandits on the ground. He checked their pockets and saw a note… He took it and looked at the note carefully and started to read the note out of the dead man's pocket: "There is no turning back from here, you better get used to, you are going to the great meeting for nothing... Blaad."

He sliced his calm attitude by losing a moment, squeezing the note in his hand, and kicking the dead body several times. He took a deep breath and calmed down again and looked around once more for the last time.

In the darkness of the night, he clenched his knees in the silent steps of his twin daggers and continued walking, talking repeatedly, "It's always because of you Blaad... Because of you!"

The Nox Crystal

U thoroughly possessed the abandoned shed he found, studied the pointed spot on the map and continued to wait for the night to be on the road, thinking "How difficult could it be..."

The pointed structure could be seen from the shed, and it was not hard to find out that this interesting structure, rising inside the forest, belonged to a magician. He visited the building a few times and watched the inside of the building from a window and without the gate and memorized the way in and out.

With a complete collapse of the darkness, the figure, which looked like a shadow out of himself, headed towards to the pointed structure without any sound, and held his twin daggers close to his belt.

He jumped at the front of the pointed structure by making a lasso which made of rope that he pulled out from the bag to the window that was open every night and checked the strength of the rope firmly by attaching it to the edge of the window. He looked around quickly and hung the daggers and began to head upwards. When he approached the window, he held his hand against the edge of the window and gently lifted his head and looked inside. As predicted, the interior was empty and there were hundreds of magical components in the room standing on the shelves of the small room.

U put himself inside the room with a masterful move around once more, on his knees and his daggers in his hands where he could be ready for everything. He did not sense any traps, and immediately went to examine the spell components on the shelves, while thinking of why he would have given the most difficult task to gather nox crystals.

He could not find the green crystals he was looking for and walked to the door of the room. Though he slowly pushed the door, a heavy sound came out of the door, and he squeezed his face and passed through the door. The voice was struck by all the tower which probably was heard by the unwanted sorcerer. So he put his ear on the wall and closed his eyes and listened to the voices. When he was sure that there were no problems, he let go of his breath and began to calm down and descend the stairs.

After one floor went down, he stood against two doors that were in a locked position and loosened the hinges of the doors with one of his daggers to prevent the doors from making noise again. He first pushed the door on the right and noticed the middle-aged sorcerer lying in his bed behind the opening door. He immediately pulled the door back and turned to the other door. He saw the shelves that were near the door and again full of magical components. He entered the room, his eyes looked for the green crystals and seeing one green crystal, he immediately took the crystal to his hands. "I think this is it..." He thought putting the crystal in the bundle, knotting the bundle, and leaving it.

The bundle was about to take off, but a force hindered the progress of the flying. The daggers, seen in U's hands, seemed to have been there from the beginning in their hands and he swiftly leaned back right after he sensed the danger. He stood in front of the sorcerer, saw that he was trying to stop the bundle with his hands, noticing that he was not letting them go, and so he threw one of his daggers to the centre of his hand of the sorcerer and interrupted his concentration.

The bundle that survived the spell flew out of the window and disappeared. After completing his task, U relieved and took a short breath and reached the dagger on the floor with a smile. The sorcerer wanted to hit to U with the bottom of his staff, but when he could not succeed, he became very tense, and he threw himself out of the room and casted an unknown spell by closing the door.

A miniature lion figure falling to the bottom of U's feet began to grow by fogging and so, U grabbed his daggers tightly and ran back into the room's wall, trapped in a tiny room with a large lion.

U realized that the lion was expecting a command from his owner, and this would be an immediate attack opportunity and he decided to make the first move to the lion. Indeed, U managed to give a small cut, and the lion was furious with it. The lion's bright eyes turned to U and got ready to the jumping position by tilting its hind legs.

U, who is always prepared for direct attacks, briefly weighed the lion, and nestled on his knees, predicting the action it will take. U, who stumbled on the lion's throat, turned on his daggers to the lion and struck them into its throat professionally in a few seconds, and the lion was quickly defeated and turned again into fog and disappeared.

After his easy-to-imagine rival, he approached toward the door to face the sorcerer, but came close to the side of the door, and opened the door by pushing it with the tip of his dagger. A flash of lightning darted inside, and the lightning bolt made sparkles by hitting the walls, missing its target.

At that exact moment, the opportunity to surprise the sorcerer arose, U clung to his knees standing in front of the door with a clap and pierced his daggers into the stomach of the sorcerer. The daggers seemed to cut through a soft velvet dress, which made U smile as he realized how defenceless the sorcerer was against the influence of his daggers.

The inanimate body fell on the ground softly, U's smile took a short time and stopped for a second and thought how he got used to the brutal massacres he did. He was not a rogue anymore, he was an assassin, a very deadly one. He said to himself, "How am I so... How am I become such a cold-blooded killer?" and looking at the dead body lying in front of him, "Please forgive me, this was not my intention, but you attacked me before..."

He did not get any answer from the dead body and U closed the eyes of the corpse, which he felt very sorry, and carried the body to its bed. Waiting at the top of the corpse, a few more minutes, he decided to return to the chateau for the meeting and climbed up, holding the rope in the window, and descending rapidly.

Between the shadows, the shady figure continued to walk to the chateau with the most silent steps...

The Obstacles

"So, you could be able to pack up the magical components... And invited everyone to your chateau..." Blaad released the crow, which watched the inside of the chateau with the eyes of it and transferred the information to Blaad. As the pressure on the crow descended, it realized that it was free and relaxed and began to fly away without even looking back.

Blaad, who was sitting in the castle, thought how to stop the great meeting and began to make plans to intervene sooner, considering the return paths of his friends to the chateau.

He did not have much choice, except for a small orc army he could buy, or a few mercenaries. He knew that these obstacles would not work very well; because his competitors have repeatedly proven that they were all tough warriors.

"I will go to the chateau first, I will defeat Behim, and I will destroy and exterminate the magic parchment..." Blaad said to himself and thought about his plans to stay alive. He was about to begin his walk, but he returned his face to his new slave and smiled sincerely, saying: "Don't worry Aridem, I will bring you to your king and queen, and when I am done, I will make sure you suffer, and make sure you rot in there, with your kind and with your queen…"

Aridem, who fell short of strength due to the teeth marks on his neck and the enchanted wrangles of his wrists, managed to lift his head and took a glance from where he was sitting, desperately...

THE LAST SPELL

The Lich

Behim gazed at himself for hours in front of the mirror, touched once more to his rotten face. Then he looked at his rotten hands again. He put his hands inside his red gown of his robe and turned his back toward his seat with slight steps.

A simple illusion could spill itself into a normal view, but he did not want to fool himself. Maybe when his friends came, he could make an illusion spell that would change his appearance to not disturb their morale or not to distress them.

But the image was not important, the result was important! He was trusting that his plan would work for him which he was working on it for a long time, but all of his friends had to unite, or at least most of them.

He looked at the ancient clock hanging on the wall and spoke to himself, "Slightly and shortly, they might arrive at any moment." He then stood in front of the mirror, walking near the mirror again, and murmuring a magic spell, sending a message to his long-suffering enemy: "Blaad! Here's the answer! Your answer! I have it! You need to come too!"

He was not sure if the message had arrived; because the castle that Blaad chose for himself was protected by robust magic, and he could not get any answer for his telepathic messages that he had sent before.

Lich Behim walked to the corner of the room, which he could only enter. The chest opened with a spell, and the phylactery in it stood slightly untouched. He took the phylactery which holds his spirit hidden and watched his own soul sinking into the phylactery. He spoke, "How did we come to this?" and put the phylactery in the chest, sealing the cover of the chest with a spell. He had been doing the same thing over and over for no reason. Maybe the reason was he had been very alone for a very long time. Even though he was an undead creature, he still needed to have some company.

He was about to pass in front of his mirror, paused by a very painful cry. He lifted his head up and watched his ghost friend Kandaz gliding through the hall. "My little old friend, I am going to fix everything…" He promised to his friend, came near to his mirror again, and looked at his rotten face. Later, his hands, which seemed to be bruised due to rotting, attracted his attention again, and immediately put his hands inside his robe.

Behim turned his face to the mirror again, diminishing his red eyes: "It was always because of you Blaad.. Always! You have always been seeking the trouble and everything is all on you!" and he continued to look at himself at the same time. His body was about to turn into a full skeleton if he had allowed to. "Why am I hiding myself?" was his thought but he did not think about it, instead he focused on his plan and wanted to be sure that it will be the solution to everything.

The Vampire Lord

The enormous castle at the very edge of the forest would catch everyone's attention from afar, but nobody would dare to approach. Traders have always preferred to pass through the woods instead of passing around the castle; the travellers have always changed their direction when they saw the castle. Even the animals in the woods were not approaching it because of the negative aura and the negative energy of the castle.

The grass around the castle was drying and rotting every day. The unnatural cursed aura, which covered every perimeter of the castle, was affecting everything that is alive around it in the worst way.

The treasure hunters who dared to approach the castle could hear some sounds of groaning, and some claimed they had seen a great wolf. The number of people who came too close to the castle and returned was very small. Those who were fortunate stepped into the castle died by a trap and those who were unfortunate stayed captive in the dungeon and could not see the day again.

But there was an excitement in the dungeon that night. An effort that had some hope in it after years.

The fallen king Boura, a long-time prisoner, broke his chains that surrounded his wrists with a last-minute effort, and took the first step to realize his dreams of an escape.

Breaking the chains created an excitement and hope for the whole group, and his wife, the queen Guen, who was attached to the same chain, got her freedom as well, smiled at Boura in a semi-unconscious way.

- "I'm coming right now, my queen!" Boura called, picking up the glass of water on the floor, lifting Guen's head and offering water to his wife. Guen, who was drinking poorly, looked around, but again fell into despair and leaned forward.

- "What will happen next? Anyway, everyone thinks we're dead. And where are we going to run away? Is there really a kingdom? What if all is a lie?" Guen started asking questions.

- "Do not tire yourself, my love, let's get out of this hell hole first, let's see the sky again, the fresh air, some real food, everything will be fine, I promise, one by one…" Boura replied.

While Boura was trying to break Guen's chains, he heard footsteps from above and immediately sat down, taking the chains behind his hands.

From the other corner of the vault, Sermut's voice was heard, suggesting his friends, "Do not worry about it, tonight is my turn..."

With the opening of the dungeon door, they all became silent and saw a new prisoner, brought in by the vampire lord Blaad.

Moving toward the empty space of the cell, Blaad hesitated for a moment and looked at Boura and blinked at him. He then looked at Guen and took a few more steps to stand in front of Airhan's cell. "It looks like your friend couldn't make it." He laughed and held the new prisoner with his arm and threw him into the cell where Airhan's dead body was found. "You will stay here for a long time, get used to it, Aridem." Talked to the spy and then he turned his head backwards and shouted at the door: "Aypher! There's a corpse to take care of! Eat it or throw it away, I don't care! Just get rid of it!"

A few minutes later, the dungeon door opened again, and the werewolf Aypher came in. Aypher looked angrily around, walked to the cell where Airhan was, and turned to Blaad: "Yes, my lord." He replied calmly.

Blaad walked to the front of the next cell and looked at the two weakened figures inside.

Blaad asked a question mockingly: "So, do you enjoy being here? My friends?"

- "Kill us…" A weak answer came from Hasun.

- "Yes, kill us, that's enough, we can't take it anymore!" An angry voice came from Aijan sitting next to him.

- "I did not come here to kill you, in fact you both look pretty good." Blaad said with laughter and asked mockingly: "And why are you always that angry?"

At that moment, by fluttering her wings of the opposite cell, "What more do you want from us? We do not have the answer you're looking for!" Yelled Ezma.

- "I know, but I need you too, and you know that we've talked about this issue so many times, over and over again…" Blaad said, pointing to the cell of Ezma.

Turning his face to the other cell, Blaad saw Ouzan lying inside the cell and said: "I sent a little orc squad to play with your brother Zegan." Ouzan's hand went straight to the waistband on his arm and stared at Blaad for a moment, then turned his head to the ceiling and drowned to thoughts again.

Blaad, who took several more steps into the depths of the basement, came to the front of Sermut's cell and opened the door of the cell. He looked at him with a pity, but then returned to Sermut. "I am afraid tonight's your turn, you know it." Blaad said, showing his vampire teeth and pulling Sermut over to him, and piercing the teeth through his neck gently. Because of the sudden pain that spreads to Sermut's body, "Dude…" was the only thing he could say before he passed by.

Blaad, who got his daily energy after consuming the fresh blood, went straight to the door without looking at anyone and stepped out, pointing at Aypher to follow him. "Do you realize it has been 11 years today?" Blaad's voice echoed to the shack, asking Aypher, and then disappeared.

Blaad and his loyal friend werewolf Aypher, whom they have trusted each other for years, have begun to walk upwards.

- "It's been 11 years!" Blaad shouted.

- "You're right, my lord, it's been 11 years... What are we up to now?" Aypher looked at him with his questioning eyes.

- "A message from Behim, claims that he found what I'm looking for and invites me to his chateau." Replied Blaad.

- "Behim?" Aypher hissed angrily, taking off his wolf teeth.

- "Yes, and I'll be going shortly." Blaad said.

- "My lord? Let me come with you." Said Aypher.

- "Do not worry my friend, and you know, nobody in this world could hurt me." He resolved his friend's unnecessary anxiety.

- "Well, did he really find it?" Aypher eagerly asked.

- "I believe in Behim. Even if it's not true, it's worth a try. At least we will have done something. You know it's been exactly 11 years today. I've been looking for Haipe for 11 years! 11 long years! Behim wouldn't lie about it, there must be something!" Blaad replied, raising his voice.

- "Haipe..." Aypher whispered sadly.

- "I'll find her. I'll find my love!" Blaad started walking toward his room, and then suddenly returned to Aypher again.

Blaad looked at the dungeon door and gave orders to Aypher, "They're going to flee soon, do not interfere, let them go." Blaad kept walking but stopped again: "Or kill them all, I don't care!"

- "As you wish my lord…" Aypher answered.

- "And before I go, I will send the book to us now, I will send it back through time, and it will reach to us, do not worry. I found a way to do this, and today is the day." Blaad said, placing a huge and insidious smile on Aypher's face.

Approaching the red door of his room, Blaad put himself in the form of a mist instead of opening the door of the room, and he floated under the door and took in the human form again. He has really been enjoying changing forms. Firstly, the book was on the table, and he looked at him with disgust. He casted a complex magic that he was working on, and the book disappeared in seconds. Then he looked at Haipe's portrait, which he had painted on the wall of the room a long time ago, and said, "They are right, it is all because of me..." and whispered, "But I will find you!" and he continued, promising at his words this time.

He turned his back, took his red dagger on the table, moved his finger to his ring and gave a kick to the door of the room and broke it into pieces.

Blaad walked angrily but decisively until the main door of the castle, stood in front of his door again and shook his friend's hand as he bid farewell to Aypher, who was waiting for him. Aypher bowed and responded to him by not saying anything but whimpering. Again, entering the mist form, Blaad leaned out of the gate of the castle, taking the human form out of the castle, stood on his feet, and looked at the long road ahead. He was sure something big was waiting him, so he turned his head back and gave another look to his castle one last time, remembering the first time he came here, then closed his eyes and concentrated on his mission.

Blaad went through the night and continued his way...

The Great Meeting

Behim, who was waiting outside of his chateau, tried to smile with the excitement of seeing his friends whom he could not see for a very long time...

Realizing that he did not use laughing muscles of his face for a very long time, Behim felt like his facial muscles were severely damaged, immobilizing his face so he quickly made it restored by a minor magic.

A voice made him turned himself around back to the chateau and immediately saw Blaad who was standing between him and the chateau, and he immediately casted himself a protection spell.

- "I did not come to attack you!" Spoke Blaad, thinking what would happen, and he created himself a protection spell as well.

- "So, you had my messages!" Yelled Behim.

Blaad's attitude: "From the very beginning!" angered Behim.

- "All of our friends are dead! And it's all because of you!" Shouted Behim.

- "Maybe... But you know, we played this game together. I mean, you have a big contribution in this too! Now, tell me, where is Haipe? Or were you lying again? Lying to me as well as to the people that we used to call friends? You are the one to be blamed, more than me!" Said Blaad and this was the last drop in the glass for Behim.

Behim, who became frustrated, turned, and pulled his right hand into the pocket of his robe, pulling out a black substance on a pinch and making a mark with his left hand, throwing that substance in the direction of a complicated spell.

Blaad watched the ground trembling and laying out a flare of fire in the flames, a few steps down, but retained his stern look. He knew that Behim had casted a dangerous conjuring spell, and he had a lot of experience in such spells, so he knew how to act against them.

The slit on the ground grew and a big black demon burst into fires with flames.

The height of the demon was probably three people tall, and his muscular arms were as wide as a body of a very fat man.

The demon ascended to the ground and strengthened his position by pressing his feet to the dirt and began to sift around his eyes.

Having received the message of "Kill him!" from Behim, the demon, obeying his master, turned to Blaad, who was standing right in front of him, but no matter how precise the order was, he could not find the courage to attack to Blaad and the demon had a fear.

Behim commanded again, "I said kill him!" but the demon did not obey, instead turned back without listening to this command and walked over to Behim to attack his master by changing the sides.

As the demon walked toward to the lich, Behim's red eyes glanced, and another fear wave gathered into the demon's body again.

Blaad, trying to control the demon, gave a command to the demon "Kill him!" But the demon could not find the courage to attack Behim too, confused and he turned back again.

Normally, a black demon, who had a mighty power to disperse an army alone, felt very weak between these two, and with his head spinning out of fear, he started casting a spell and began to disappear with flames. His intention was sending himself back to hell where he could be away from them!

Behim shouted "No!" and he took the control again and called the demon back from his disappearing demolition.

The demon, who rebelled and screamed and flashed around himself, was summoned back, and began to look at Behim with disgust and hatred.

At that moment, the demon, aware of a flying person towards him from his upper side, lifted his arm to the point where he could defend himself.

The demon, although strong, did not have the reflexes to protect himself for the sudden attacks, and there was nothing he could do to prevent a sword with divine powers from having broken his skull.

The demon, which first stopped rigidly, turned to ashes and the flames began to fade, then disappeared by leaving a black smoke.

Monem thanked Dhammal, who threw himself into the air, and then stood on the road between the deadly rivals.

Looking at Blaad in a long and meaningful way, Monem took his sword again and walked beside Behim and stood side by side with Behim.

In the same way, Dhammal went after Monem and moved to the other side of Behim, grabbing his war hammer and looking angrily at Blaad.

- "I congratulate you... You chose to be on the same level with a lich..." Said Blaad.

- "This lich, on the contrary, is struggling for all of us for years! He is trying to fix everything while you are making it complicated! For 11 years Blaad! 11 years!" Answered Monem.

Dhammal, asking questions by whispering, "Has it only been that long?" spoke to himself without blinking his eyes. His face would be the answer that Blaad's eyes clamped to them.

- "You promised that you would give me the answer! Where is Haipe?" Asked Blaad, though angry, was hard to smile at the irony created by a lich and a paladin standing side by side.

- "Haipe could not come to this world you fool! Because of you, she could not stay in our own world either! She is squeezed between! And for years, she's been flying within those planes with the ones that have been lost, like herself!" The answer that Behim gave to Blaad made his face in a terrible condition.

- "How? Where is that plane? How are we going to save her?" Blaad asked.

- "There is no salvation for her! She will stay there forever, and these are just because of you!" Behim shouted, then started laughing because of the complexity of Blaad's feelings. He knew they were winning.

- "Why are you calling me here for then? To tell me this? To see me suffer? To mock me? You will see!" Blaad hissed.

Blaad, with both hands sideways, casted a spell and sent a large fireball aiming to the head of Behim.

Behim raised his arms in a way that made the rotten hands open and formed a magic shield covering his friends. The great fireball crashed into Behim's magic shield and went off on it.

Following the events that had been happening, Blaad smiled sneakily and held out his hands forward and threw a lightning bolt towards Behim's foot. The lightning proceeded in a noisy and swift manner, smashing Behim to the soil and breaking the magic shield and throwing the three of them backwards.

Blaad's smile, aware of the panic read by Behim's face, grew, and began to shake his hands to send a new fireball right in the middle of the group that were trying to get up. This time he was going to hit his defenceless targets.

Blaad noticed the incoming twin daggers flying right at that last moment, and he was able to prevent the daggers by turning his spell into a protection spell.

U's right on time reunion rescued their friends' lives, but this time Blaad, who lifted the daggers with a telekinesis spell, threw his daggers back to U, and now U's life was in danger.

U felt the wind of his daggers while clinging to his knees, the daggers flew over his head, and the only thing that kept U from the daggers that looked like bullets was the agility and the lightning reflexes of U again.

With a quick manoeuvre, U found himself standing next to Monem, and this time four of them stood side by side, turned to Blaad, and cautioned against the attacks that might come.

- "I see that you know how to survive..." Blaad said, causing U to be angry.

- "I've always waited for this day…" Spoke U and spiked his teeth and started to look for an opportunity to attack Blaad again.

- "We are alive... but all our friends are dead!" Said Monem, showing his waistband on his arm.

- "There are other survivors, too..." Said Blaad and "Maybe it was better than death, but anyway..." he continued, grinning.

- "Yes, there are other survivors too!" Said Behim, taking out the magic parchment in his pocket and showing it to Blaad.

- "Zjan..." Whispered Blaad and thought for a moment, but then he began to get serious: "Are you begging me so much to go back?"

- "We will go back! We will go back to the date where we came from!" Answered Behim.

- "And you will not remember anything!" Dhammal said, lifting his head and laughing.

- "But we'll remember everything…" Continued Monem, who then gave a look at Blaad with menacing impression with his face.

- "What do you think will happen when you return? I think we were in a much better world than before?" Blaad asked.

- "At least our friends were alive!" U looked around and answered, "We were also at peace...".

- "I will tell you what will happen when we return... There will be hard-working life, earning money, boring and routine days... Did you forget about these things? Are you leaving this place and choosing such a miserable life?" Blaad explained, but the group was apparently speaking out of sight.

- "We are going back, and you are coming with us! There is no debate!" Said Dhammal, looking at Behim to start the magic.

There was no trace of anxiety or fearful look on Blaad's face. There was something in Blaad's laughing with the answer to Behim, feeling something might go wrong:

- "Do you remember the book? The book that I found with Aypher? The book that two people brought? The book, which is supposedly you were working on?" Blaad was pleased with the expressions of the face of his friends.

- "What? What happened to the book?" Behim asked nervously.

- "I was the one who sent the book, you fool! I have sent it to our world and the book has already reached to us, to me! Even if you do this now, it will not work..." Blaad said with a frown, "Maybe it will work for you, but because the book will go back to the past, and we will repeat these things forever... So, if you read that scroll, you will make everything worse, you will trap us into a loop!"

With Blaad's words, everybody covered a deep silence, and everybody began to think about what was said...

- "Could it be true, Behim?" Asked Monem.

- "Somehow... But there is something he does not know. This magic will not only lead us to the time and place we came. Only those who are here now will remember what is happening, but those who are not here will not remember anything. Moreover, they will go to different venues and some of them will never even meet us... So, it will not be possible for this group to go to the house party!" Behim explained.

- "Are you sure, Behim?" Dhammal asked uneasily.

- "I am sure! It must be! Imagine, even if the book comes to Blaad as he claims, there will be no meaning because the people who come to this party will never have met and most of the old things will never have happened." Behim explained.

- "So, is this really such a powerful magic?" Asked Monem, rolling his eyes suspiciously on the magic parchment.

- "Yes, perhaps the strongest!" Said Behim eagerly.

Listening and assimilating the spoken words, Blaad felt a feeling he had not felt for a long time: Fear! But he gained control in a short time and relied on his powers to overcome this feeling.

Blaad asked, "And how do you think that I will let you read this magic scroll?" He did not want to do it, but the only solution was to kill them. Maybe it was too late for this...

- "I know you will not let me! That's why I brought someone with me!" Behim shouted, making a sign with his hand and a word of magic sprouting from the balcony of the chateau.

Recognizing the melodic voice that came, Blaad turned toward the balcony, cursed himself for not being able to sense it before, and remained motionless against the enchanting spell, unable to prevent the incoming spell.

"Forgive me cousin Blaad... But it is necessary for us to go back..." Zjan spoke, approving Behim.

With Blaad's paralysis, Behim opened his magic parchment to his front and started to read the scroll...

The Very Last Spell

- "Nobody moves from this place! No one makes a sound! Anything that might disrupt the concentration of Behim will be deadly! Let's be prepared for anything!" Monem said, withdrawing his shield from his back and leading himself to Behim.

- "But you are talking, but..." U remembered his ability of sense of humour which he has not used for years.

Dhammal was very excited with his knees trembled: "We are at home soon!"

Zjan was struggling to keep Blaad from getting free. Feeling that Blaad's resistance was growing stronger, Zjan quietly talked to Behim: "Please make it fast, please..."

Behim of course did not hear what Zjan said, because he was in a state of full concentration for the magic. The voice of the lich was occasionally descended, sometimes rising, and his hands were drawing signs in the air. The magical parchment stood in the air just opposite to Behim, and the words of the magic written on the scroll were disappearing once read.

It was quite too long to finish!

Behim's voice lifted so suddenly that Monem standing in front of him had left his shield and had to close his ears only with both hands. Then Dhammal and U collapsed and closed their ears too.

Zjan, whose ears were already fragile, could not resist the rising loud voice and was baffled by the moment he was holding Blaad. He lost his control over Blaad and panicked.

Recognizing that he was released, Blaad thought to run to Behim first, but then he realized Behim was coming to the last words of the scroll and understood that he did not have enough time. He thought that he could manipulate the spell that was being done, and quickly casted back a spell to Behim, creating the last and dispelling spell.

After the last word disappeared, the magic scroll burned itself in the air, and Behim and Blaad looked at each other. Neither of them had the slightest idea that the magic they casted was worked.

However, the fog that started to form in front of Behim proved that Behim had succeeded in his magic.

The group that accepts the fog, happily hugged them, left them with an empty eye and began to disappear one by one. First, Monem, then U and Dhammal, and finally Zjan disappeared in the mist.

The empty gaze in the eyes of those lost in the mist caused Behim's face to turn to Blaad in panic. Behim realised something went wrong, a very minor detail went wrong!

"The last spell I made is worked! I will remember everything... But you guys are not going to remember anything! I will come back! I will!" Blaad started laughing, revealing the vampire teeth, and not blocking the smile spreading in his face.

The fog covered Blaad too and Blaad's laughter was unheard of.

Finally, the fog that covered all also took Behim and the magic sent them to the world which they all belonged to...

Back to Home

Everything happened like what was written on the magic parchment...

The only person who remembered everything was Blaad and that was happened thanks to the last spell made by Blaad...

The most surprising thing about Blaad, who found himself near the antique fountain and on his knees, was the breath he had. He went to the point that he had to air his lungs, which he had not used to this for a long time. Later, he checked his teeth immediately and his face was hung when he realized that his vampire teeth had gone.

The first rays of the sun, which was hitting to his face, began to grow and he watched the sunrise as he narrowed his eyes.

He moaned with his groaning voice from his side and saw Dhammal lying on the ground. He immediately held his watch on Dhammal's arm and looked straight at it. It was "18 May 2005" at the time.

He looked around and saw Behim, Monem, U, and Zjan. They were all lying down on the ground.

There was no information about the fate of the other friends. As Behim pointed out, the others were in different places, and they did not even remember what was happening, and they had no news at all. Some of them has not even met yet!

- "It was really a powerful spell..." Said Blaad and suddenly turned his back with a hand touching his shoulder.

- "Indeed, it was a very powerful spell..." Dhammal laughed and caused Blaad's eyes to grow.

- "You remember!" Blaad said, breathing.

- "I remember the drinks I had! Look, we've been out here all night!" Dhammal laughed and laughed, saying: "It was a really powerful spell! Ha-ha!"

- "You do not remember..." Blaad said breathing.

- "Really, what are we doing here? Why did we come here? Did we really sleep here all the night?" Dhammal asked.

- "I do not know..." Said Blaad, realizing his awakening friends.

Monem leaned over from the floor and began to rub his head with his hands saying: "My head..."

- "What have you done to me again, Blaad?" Asked Monem and looked around.

- "Nothing..." Blaad replied silently.

- "Oh, my stomach, did I eat the whole package of the crisps again?" Monem complained.

- "No idea…" Replied Blaad again, whispering.

- "Are you okay? You also look so bad." Asked Monem again.

- "I'm fine, I just have a little pain in my head... Don't worry about me." Said Blaad.

A few minutes passed and U and Zjan woke up in turn.

- "Look, we slept all night long!" U stood up and everyone turned to him.

- "What did we do last night?" Zjan scratched his ear and straightened his hair.

- "The last time we were at home, we went out to get some air... I do not remember then." U replied.

Blaad felt like puking on himself by hearing these none-sense conversations, and he wanted to do another test to check on the spell which he casted to make sure:

- "Sermut?" Asked Blaad.

- "What? Who?" Dhammal asked.

- "Boura? Guen?" Asked Blaad again.

- "What are you talking about?" Said Monem.

- "Ezma? Hasun? Mourem?" Asked Blaad and again.

- "Cousin Blaad, are you okay? Who are they?" Asked Zjan.

- "How many people were in our house yesterday?" Blaad asked one last question.

- "All of us, cousin Blaad, we all here." Zjan replied.

- "He must have hit his head very hard!" Laughed Dhammal but was ignored.

Another question from Blaad: "And what did we do?"

- "It was good, so we ate, we drank, and we had fun... What could we do?" Zjan answered.

After this answer, Blaad, satisfied, looked at the antique fountain and watched the flowing waters for a while.

- "Friends, I think Blaad does not feel very well." Said Monem, who came to the fountain and rubbed his face with a handful of water flowing through the fountain.

- "Are you okay, Cousin Blaad? Do you need anything else?" Zjan asked but could not get a response.

- "Blaad, tell me something, do you not feel good? Do you need something?" A question came from Monem.

- "Could you please call Haipe?" Blaad asked, thinking that he had not used his phone for years in his pocket.

- "Well…" Said Monem, settled on his hands, dialled the number, and handed the phone to Blaad.

Blaad put the phone on his ear, and he smiled, breathing comfortably at the voice he had not heard for 11 years saying to him: "Good morning... Are you okay?" Blaad breathed again and said: "I'm fine, I just wanted to hear your voice... That's why I called..." He hung up the phone and put the phone in his pocket.

Dhammal's voice "Behim is about to wake up." suddenly turned Blaad toward Behim.

Behim woke up and opened his eyes slowly. Behim looked around with lively eyes instead of red eyes, stretched his mouth wide open and said: "Oh brother, what a night it was!"

Everyone laughed and then gathered near Blaad, who was standing next to the fountain.

Blaad tried to get himself together by squeezing his fists, approaching Behim first and gazing at him with a hateful look and then yelled at everyone: "I'll meet them again! I will enter back to their lives somehow! And while you do not know anything, I'll find a way back!"

After a few silent moments, Blaad quietly looked at the faces of his friends who had no idea about the subject, saying, "The party is over..." for the last time.

Blaad bowed his head in front of him and began to walk slowly to his home...

THE LAST WORD

Blaad, who once again looked at the books in his hand:

- "Do you know what the most interesting thing about this?" Blaad continued, saying: "No one will remember anything, and if they read this book, they will only think that they read a fantasy novel..."

- "Why do you want them to remember anyway?" Asked the dark figure.

- "I want them to know what's happened. I want them to know who they were. And maybe... I want forgiveness... I was so unfair. I cannot even look into the eyes of some..." Blaad responded by nodding his head.

- "They will never believe you..." Said the dark figure.

- "Yes, nobody will believe... But maybe, maybe someone remembers it?" Blaad lifted his head with hope.

- "No, it is not possible." Said the dark figure, ending the debate clearly.

The dark figure stood up and looked out of the window.

- "I do not understand how you live in this world..." He spoke.

- "We have no other choice..." Blaad replied.

- "Soon, a few years later, there will be fires, earthquakes, wars…" The dark figure continued: "And the most lethal pandemics which will wipe some of you out from the earth unfortunately…"

- "What pandemics?" Asked Blaad with questioning eyes…

- "Just take care of yourself and your loved ones…" Whispered the dark figure and stopped suddenly.

- "You know that I really hate when you start talking in riddles!" Blaad said, rolling his eyes.

- "Never mind… I talked enough!" Was the only reply from the dark figure.

- "We have no other choice..." Blaad replied again with hopeless eyes after some time.

Against this answer, the dark figure looked out again. Then he turned his head to Blaad.

- "You know you can come whenever you want, don't you?" Asked the dark figure.

- "Yes... But I will not return." Blaad answered quietly.

- "Well then..." Said the head of the dark figure with the cloak and said, "Farewell Blaad..." with a smile that reveals his vampire teeth.

- "Goodbye, Blaad..." Blaad approached him and shook his hand hard.

Later, Blaad gave way to the vampire. The vampire Blaad crossed the mirror in the room, casted a spell, and disappeared by touching the mirror with his finger.

After the vampire's departure, Blaad looked at the books that he just wrote and looked at himself for a while on the mirror. Then he left his room to give the books to his friends to find out...

THE END

Printed in Great Britain
by Amazon

37247862R00071